The Discreet Charm Of Mary Maxwell-Hume

Gordon Lawrie

Comely Bank Publishing

First published 2017 by Comely Bank Publishing

ISBN: 978-0-9930262-6-3

Original cover design by Learmonth Designs
Text printed in Adobe Garamond Pro by 4edge Limited

A CIP catalogue record for this book is available from
the British Library.

For Bruce Levine, who insisted that these
stories be written.

CONTENTS

INTRODUCTION

Mary Maxwell-Hume was never a character I really gave a lot of thought to in the first place. I'd written a novel, *Four Old Geezers And A Valkyrie* and, as kind of 'hook', I wrote a short story called *The Piano Exam* as a prequel to the novel itself. It was always intended to be a giveaway, but of course Amazon had to spoil that making a minimum charge. All I was trying to do was to introduce my central character to potential readers, and in particular to my writing style. In addition, *The Piano Exam*, like *Four Old Geezers And A Valkyrie*, was written in the first person and in present tense: I wanted to readers to have the chance to see if they could deal with that. If you haven't read *The Piano Exam*, it's at the very end of this book as a little bonus, although to match the the rest of the book it's been re-written in the past tense. But the nine tales that make up *The Discreet Charm of Mary Maxwell-Hum*e technically end at *Christmas*.

The story was already five years old and had been snapped up by hundreds of readers (it was free, after all), when I found myself corresponding with Bruce Levine. Bruce is a native Manhattenite now living in Florida. He'd submitted some flash fiction – ultra-short stories – to a website called Friday Flash Fiction that I edit. Bruce is actually a well-known musician, musical director and composer, as well as possessing many other skills in theatre, writing and the arts.

So I sent him *The Piano Exam* for his entertainment.

Bruce loved the story, but even more, he loved Mary Maxwell-Hume, the 'other' character in *The Piano Exam*. He urged to me write more about her exploits, and this short volume of nine stories about this sensuously loveable rogue of a woman is the result. The first two are written in the third person, but in the third tale Mary 'acquires' an assistant: a young police constable. From then on, the remaining stories are told from his point of view.

I hope you enjoy them.

Gordon Lawrie
July 2017

THE LOGAN

'Hmm…'

The woman was peering at a painting that was around four feet wide and three feet tall. A nervous-looking member of the security staff was studying her as she leaned further and further towards the wall. Jim watched anxiously as, without taking her eyes off the painting, she slipped her hand down into her deep red leather handbag. Did she have a knife? Or a pen? A can of spray paint? His colleague should have searched her bag at Lambert's entrance, but Bomber Brown was on the door this shift and he was as idle as they come. Just the previous week Bomber had been employed as an agency guard at the Sheriff Court and failed to spot someone bringing a camcorder into the main court to film the entire proceedings as Mad Malky Morrison had been sent down for thirty years for a Glasgow gangland killing.

Still leaning impossibly like the Tower of Pisa, the woman emerged with… a gold lorgnette. Utterly confused, and clueless as to the woman's intentions, Jim was about to summon assistance when the woman lifted the gold-rimmed reading glasses to squint at the label more closely. He relaxed, realising that the woman was simply unable to read without assistance.

'Were you worried?' she asked, still not taking moving her gaze from the canvas. 'I'm so sorry.'

'No, no, it's all right,' Jim lied. He felt uncomfortable, sweating a little in difficult places under his uniform. The woman wore a black, sheer crepe dress which flowed effortlessly across her form from her shoulders to around

1

the middle of her calf. It showed very little, but somehow managed to reveal everything. He knew he shouldn't be doing it, but he found himself imagining what else she might be wearing, and couldn't come up with much of an answer. Apart from her perfume that was; something subtle, ancient, penetrating and lingering – and probably expensive.

'What do you think?' she asked.

'Sorry?' Jim wanted her to leave and wanted her stay all at once.

'What do you think?' she repeated. She smiled serenely. 'The Logan.'

Jim managed to pull himself together briefly. 'Sorry, Miss – I mean Madam. I'm afraid I don't know much about art. I only work here.'

The woman's eyebrows shot up. 'My,' she said, with a wry chuckle, 'that could almost be Lambert's motto – 'I don't know much about art, I only work here.' I wonder what the Latin for that is?'

'Sorry?'

'Never mind,' the woman said, reassuringly. 'It doesn't matter. And you were right first time…, Jim,' she added, now using her lorgnette for the first time in his direction to read his name-badge. 'I am a 'Miss'.'

'Sorry, Miss, it's none of my business.'

'Don't apologise. We nuns are proud of our profession.'

'Nun?' Jim was now back in full-on confusion mode as he studied the black figure with the scarlet handbag.

'I serve the Sisters of Mary of the Sacred Cross,' she explained.

'I've never heard of them,' Jim confessed. 'I thought nuns wore habits, or whatever they're called.'

'We *do* sometimes wear red habits. You might have seen

us around the city?'

Jim pondered for a moment, then admitted, 'Sorry, I don't believe I have.' It always paid to be honest with a woman of God, he decided.

'We believe in wearing only as much as is necessary to preserve our modesty,' the woman said, slightly at a tangent. Jim could do with as few tangents as possible at that moment. The woman was still leaning somewhat in the direction of the Logan, and briefly glanced at her back to see if she was in fact supported by wires from behind.

'Do you like it?' she smiled, invitingly.

Jim looked away quickly. 'Sorry. Do I like what?'

'Take a look at what you can see, Jim. Do you like it? Yes or no?'

Jim gulped. 'Yes.'

'You prefer this to his Grey Period?'

'Grey Period?' Slowly, Jim realised that the woman was referring to the painting again. 'Sorry. I really don't know much about art. I get a bit confused.'

'Walter Logan was one of the Dundee Circle of painters, Jim. They painted in the 1920s and 1930s around the same time as the Scottish Colourists – Peploe, Hunter and so on. Have you heard of them?'

Jim shook his head. To be honest, he was still somewhat distracted by the woman's Leaning Tower impersonation.

'The Colourists were very influenced by French Impressionists, Jim. They used lots of bright colour to paint still life, ladies in bright dresses and so on. The Dundee Circle thought that was dishonest. Life in the industrial city of Dundee at the time was drab, so they painted instead in browns and greys. They weren't so successful, unfortunately. People preferred pretty things then. But the Dundee Circle are very desirable now.' She managed to infuse the word 'desirable' with a certain something that emanated from her entire being.

Jim was all at sea, 'You seem to know a lot about the painting, Miss,' he said in desperation. 'As I said, I really don't know much about art.'

'This is from Logan's Brown Period, Jim. At least that what the label there says.' Then after a moment she added, 'But I don't blame you for being confused. Whatever else this is, it's not a Logan Brown Period. Did someone switch the label while you weren't looking?'

It shook Jim out of what might have passed for a reverie. 'Certainly not, Miss...'

'Maxwell-Hume. Mary Maxwell-Hume. Licensed to verify paintings. And this is definitely *not* a Logan Brown Period. In fact I'm all but sure that it's not a Logan at all. It's a copy, a clever copy, but it's a copy. Are you sure no one switched the labels?'

'Not on my shift, Miss Maxwell...'

'Hume. Call me Mary if it's easier. Sister Mary if you like.'

'Not on my shift, Sister Mary. Mind you, I only came on an hour ago. It was that Aziz before me and he's just a young lad, he doesn't take his responsibilities as seriously as me.'

'There you go then, Jim. A weak link. Don't you think we should call the management?'

Theodore Plews – who would have been known as 'Teddy' to his friends if only he'd had any – was an unpleasant little bald man in his late fifties who seemed to think a Hitler moustache suited him. In his five years as Director at the Edinburgh branch of Lambert's Auction House, he'd had to deal with all sorts of troublemakers, but women always brought out the worst in him. He strutted towards the scene in irritation: when he saw it was Mary Maxwell-Hume standing beside Jim at the Logan, he cursed silently under his breath.

Plews' default tone of voice was 'abrupt'. 'Yes?'

Mary Maxwell-Hume smiled, but said nothing. Instead, Jim was left to do the explaining.

'Sir, this lady's been studying the picture for a good while. She's…'

Mary decided it was time to help him out. Addressing Plews, she said, '"The lady' – I – have some concerns about this picture, Mr… You haven't introduced yourself yet, by the way.'

'Theodore J. Plews. Director of Lambert's Auction House.' Then, as an afterthought, he sneered, 'And who am I speaking to?' He was faintly aware that the woman might be wearing some sort of perfume. He didn't offer his hand.

'Mary Maxwell-Hume. How nice to meet you, Mr Plews,' Mary said sweetly, offering the back of her hand for Plews to kiss. When he ignored her, she made her distaste clear, even although the words that came from her mouth would suggest otherwise. 'Mr Plews, am I to understand that this is Lot 64 from the art sale that Lambert's are due to hold tomorrow?'

'The Carberry Estate sale, yes,' Plews said. 'Are you in the market, Miss… Maxwell-Hume?'

'Well I'd be interested in any Logan, or indeed any of the Dundee Circle's work for that matter. I do find them so genuine, don't you?'

'I'm glad you like it. You'll see from the catalogue that it has a guide price of £8,000. We can look forward to seeing you tomorrow, then?' Plews knew it wasn't going to be that simple, though. Whenever he felt pressured, a nervous tic developed in the left corner of his mouth; it made his moustache shake quite visibly. His moustache was vibrating now.

'As I said,' Mary repeated, 'I'm interested in Dundee Circle art work, but this isn't Dundee Circle. It's probably not a Logan, either. It's something else. Let's be kind and say it's a copy, shall we?'

Theodore Plews said nothing for a moment, then he folded his arms. He decided to take a patronising approach.

'Well, now, Miss Maxwell-Hume… so what makes you think this isn't what it claims to be?'

'I'm surprised that a man who claims to know so much about art has to ask that question,' Mary said sharply. 'Do I *really* need to take you through it?' She glanced in the general direction of Jim to remind Plews that any humiliation would be public.

The Director weighed up his options, and decided that the woman posed little threat.

'Go on.' Plews didn't do smirks: he couldn't quite make his lips bend enough. Jim looked on with interest, though, as Mary drew herself up to her full height, which allowed her to look down on Plews' bald head from slightly above.

'Well, Mr Plews, I *am* disappointed,' she sighed. 'I'd have thought anyone with the first knowledge of the Dundee Circle would be aware that Logan never used brown after 1928.'

Plews cocked his head aggressively. 'I'd agree. This is dated 1926. So?'

'This wasn't painted in 1926, for sure.'

'Oh? And what makes you so sure of that?' The little man's face was scarred with contempt, but the twitching moustache gave away tell-tale signs of worry.

'You'll have noticed the canvas,' Mary said.

'Canvas?'

'*Factories At Dawn* is painted on coarse-grained canvas – and of course he obtained his canvasses from Donald's of Dundee, who were capable of weaving local jute into the material.'

'Of course,' Plews said. In fact, he hadn't a clue what Logan's canvasses were made of, but he wasn't admitting that.

'This, you can see by looking close up, uses four-ounce jute on the warp, and three-ounce jute on the weft. Can you see that? There's clear difference in the vertical and horizontal threading in the weave – the warp is heavier.' Mary stood back for a moment to let Plews look more closely. Then she added, 'Can you see that, Jim?'

Jim peered closely at the canvass. 'Is that those textured lines at one-inch intervals in both directions?'

'Well spotted, Jim – we'll make an art connoisseur of you yet. Can you see it Mr Plews?' Plews waved away the offer of Mary's lorgnette.

'Of course, of course.' Plews wasn't sure what he was supposed to be looking at, but he wasn't about to admit that Jim was better at spotting art detail than he was.

Mary moved in for the kill. 'The thing is, Mr Plews, you of all people will be aware that Donald's of Dundee didn't manufacture any mixed-fibre canvasses before 1931. He never painted on this type of canvas in his grey period at all. This is brown period, so…'

Plews was unsure whether to be angry, or to try to dismiss the strange woman. He was a getting confused, becoming increasingly aware of her perfume. 'Are you saying this is a fake, Miss Maxwell-Hume?'

'I'm saying that this painting is not as advertised in your

catalogue. Beyond that I can't say.'

'You seem to be remarkably knowledgeable, Miss Maxwell-Hume,' Plews said. He'd re-grouped now. 'We had this painting valued and verified by an expert, Professor John Adam of Edinburgh University. Why should I believe you over him?'

'Because Adam is a generalist,' Mary said. 'I am the true specialist in the Dundee Circle.'

'What gives you the right to claim that?'

'This, perhaps?' replied Mary, digging down into her large handbag once again to produce a small glossy-covered paperback. The cover read

The Dundee Circle
Mary Maxwell-Hume

At the foot of the page, a banner was printed: 'NOW TRANSLATED INTO ELEVEN LANGUAGES.'

'You wrote this?' Plews said, surprised. Then he remembered who he was and turned on the contempt tap again. '*I've* never heard of it. Or you, for that matter, Miss Maxwell-Hume.'

'Well, of course, Mr Plews, if you're happy, that's all that matters. I'm only trying to help. You'll be the one that's sued by any buyer who discovers that the painting on the wall isn't what it claims to be.'

'I'm prepared to take that chance,' said Plews, smugly.

'As you wish,' Mary said. 'But I'd have thought that one fairly insignificant picture was hardly worth taking any sort of chance, given the overall size and value of the Carberry estate, wouldn't you agree? I'm sure the sellers would prefer to see that their property was sold correctly.'

'Was there anything else, Miss Maxwell-Hume?' said Plews, ignoring Mary's question. 'I presume you'll not be here for the sale tomorrow?' It was said as an order.

'Of course not, Mr Plews,' said Mary. 'I'm only interested in the work of the Dundee Circle, and Logan in particular. So, no, there's nothing that interests me here.'

She turned, and gracefully made her way across the room towards the exit. Only then did Plews identify Mary's perfume: Chanel No.5.

Next day, Lambert's auctioned off 132 lots from the art collection of the Carberry estate. Theodore Plews was relieved to see that, true to her word, Mary Maxwell-Hume was nowhere to be seen. He didn't like female art experts: they made him feel uncomfortable.

When Lot 64 came up, it was announced by David Cockburn, the auctioneer for the day, as '*Factories At Dawn* by Walter Logan, oil on canvas, 1926.' It was – by the standards of the rest of the sale – a low-value lot, and Cockburn had to bang his gavel a couple of times to grab the audience's attention. He was about to set off when a hand rose in the audience to ask a question.

'Excuse me, can I seek a little clarification on something?' It was an elderly gentleman, tall and distinguished-looking with silver hair. Wearing a sports jacket and tie, he stood out slightly from many of the professional suited figures standing around who had come to bid for some valuable items which were sure to be good investments.

The auctioneer realised that the elderly gentleman was inexperienced and nodded encouragingly. 'Please sir, go ahead.'

'I've heard a rumour that the picture you're about to auction might not be all it seems. Do we have any protection if we buy?'

Across the room, a younger, bearded man piped up, 'I've actually heard that, too.'

Some thirty or so heads in prime bidding positions in the centre of the room turned from the elderly gentleman towards the younger bearded man, and back again. Then as one they turned towards the auctioneer, to see what would happen next.

The auctioneer seemed relaxed enough. 'I've had no information to suggest that Lot 64 isn't as described,' he said, peering over his reading glasses at the audience.

'I don't mean to be impertinent, but I think that picture's provenance is being questioned now,' said the bearded man. 'It's one thing to auction some item and get it wrong accidentally, but wouldn't it be fraud if you knew it was a fake?'

The auctioneer drew himself up. 'Are you suggesting that Lot 64 is a fake, sir?'

'No,' said the bearded man. 'I'm asking you if Lot 64 has been subjected to independent verification by Lambert's.'

The auctioneer picked up his telephone: Theodore Plews was on the auction floor within thirty seconds, his face scarlet with anger.

'This damned picture!' he said as burst through the door. 'Who's causing trouble now? Is it that woman again?' He stopped to look around, but he could see no sign of Mary Maxwell-Hume. Curiously, he was sure someone in the room was wearing Chanel No.5.

Many of the bidders were shocked by Plews' behaviour; a

couple actually walked out there and then, audibly muttering about the Director's rudeness – and misogyny.

A third bidder – a little hunch-backed lady in her late seventies – raised her hand to speak. The auctioneer spotted her and, teacher-like, invited her to speak.

'Excuse me…' She had a slightly nervous, quietly clipped accent that might have once been South African. She stood, blinking at Plews in an inquiring manner, with her dark red raincoat hanging open. 'I understand that you're the Director. Perhaps now that now you're here, you can vouch personally for the painting? If all of us here heard you vouch for this painting's authenticity with your own personal money rather than Lambert's, we'd all be satisfied.' She smiled sweetly, although her hunchback meant that she had to twist her head slightly to allow the smile to be seen. Plews stood speechless, so she added, 'How does that sound? Hmm?'

Plews felt his collar a tightening a little. At times like these a couple of veins stood out a little on his forehead.

'You want me to underwrite the risk personally?'

'Why not?' the woman in red said. 'You're the boss here, aren't you?' Then she added, 'Assuming you insist this is a Logan, of course.' She could see Plews struggling to maintain control of things.

'Or perhaps we could just sell it as 'unattributed'?' suggested the hunch-backed lady in the red coat. 'It could be 'sold as seen', and those who thought it was by… this Logan 'chappie' could simply take their chance.' She waved vaguely, cocked her head and smiled again. 'Personally I haven't a clue. I think it's a miserable-looking thing myself.'

Plews was aware that the Carberry estate sale was going well; most lots had realised far in excess of their anticipated value. He could have withdrawn the painting from sale, but this Logan – or whatever it was, he was beginning to wonder now – was a relatively minor item. Lambert's had a reputation for its 'White Glove sales', disposing of every single lot up for sale. He was anxious to get on with the rest of day.

'Go ahead, we've got more important things to be concerned about.' he grunted at the auctioneer. The auctioneer shrugged his shoulders, although inwardly he was embarrassed by Lambert's lack of professionalism.

Now 'sold as seen' the bidding began low, and in truth the room was slightly unsettled by the unseemly debate over the 'Logan'. Only two people bid, and the picture was knocked down at £450 to the inexperienced elderly gentleman. He went forward immediately with his chequebook, and it had to be explained to him that the payment process could wait until a gap in the proceedings. One or two of the others let out a snigger, including the bearded man who in turn found himself being upbraided by the hunch-back lady in the red coat for being 'cruel and superior'.

Seven months later, a Walter Logan painting called *Factories At Dawn* sold for just over £15,000 at the Glasgow rooms of Lambert's Auction House. The seller, Henry Dougall, was delighted, having picked up the painting for just £450 in a similar auction in Edinburgh. A gentle man, as well as a gentleman, the money had come at a good time for Dougall. Recently widowed, he'd spent the previous three years paying for his wife's nursing care in a nearby, but rather expensive, home: he'd much rather have cared for at home, but the demands of her Alzheimer's Disease had simply overwhelmed him. On her death, he'd been sent an unexpected bill for several thousand pounds, money he wouldn't have been able to raise without selling his house.

Lenny Roebuck was a man in his mid-thirties. For a few years Roebuck had sported a neat beard, the one good thing he'd picked up from a spell in Saughton Prison where he'd spent thirty months after being caught up in tax evasion scam. As the company accountant, he'd been held most responsible by the judge, even although he'd tried to say that he'd only been following instructions. Accountants who have been jailed for fraud often have difficulty once they've served their sentence, the more so since Roebuck's error had cost him his marriage as well as his profession. He, too, was a man in need of financial help.

The auction that day had been notable for the presence of a nun, unusual in itself, but doubly so because she wore a scarlet red habit that clung to every last crevice of her tall, slim form. Some onlookers expressed surprise that a nun should be so interested in art, then went on to compliment her dress, to which she replied rather enigmatically that her order believed that nuns should only wear what was necessary to preserve modesty. The nun had been rather a distracting and perfumed influence: as she drifted up nearby, several male bidders had made slightly excitable bids, driving up the eventual sale price of the lot. The Logan had been the main beneficiary.

No one complained, though.

Shortly after the Glasgow Lambert's sale, Dougall and Roebuck could be found seated at a table opposite each other in a smart new cafe in the city's Byers Road. They chatted for several minutes, but abruptly rose to their feet as the red-robed nun floated in to join them.

'That went well,' the nun said. 'Are you happy, Henry?'

'Delighted,' the older man said. 'I won't need to move house now.'

'You understand why I felt it was better to come to Glasgow,' she said. 'We didn't really want to arouse Mr Plews' suspicions, did we? And he's on holiday this week as well – studying World War 2 East Anglian airfields, or some other warlike thing. Are all men the same?'

'We're not all the same, Mary,' Roebuck reassured her.

'I'm relieved to hear it, Leonard.'

'And thank you for helping me with my own financial difficulties.'

'But the money's not all mine, is it?' Dougall said. He drew out his chequebook. 'Of our fourteen thousand pounds' profit, I understand that Lenny and I can take five thousand pounds each, is that what we agreed?'

Roebuck smiled.

'Indeed,' said the nun, 'and the remaining four thousand are my... expenses, you understand. Two books needed to be printed, for instance. And in terms of dress... a woman must maintain standards.'

'Of course.' Neither of the men was ever going to argue.

As Dougall handed the two cheques over, Roebuck said to the nun, 'Henry and I wanted to give you a present to thank you.'

'Oh, but you shouldn't – '

'You're not an easy person to buy a gift for, Mary, I won't deny it,' Roebuck said. 'You don't seem to... wear the trappings of wealth very much.' The nun lowered her eyes coyly. 'So Henry and I hope you'll accept this instead,' he added, placing a small box on the table in front of them.

The nun opened the box carefully. Could it be? Yes... a bottle of Chanel No.5.

'Ah,' she said. 'My favourite. However did you know?'

FUGUE AND OTHER ARTS

Lambert's might have been an old-established Edinburgh firm, but it wasn't old-fashioned. While other auctioneers traded on tradition and decaying style, Lambert's had long held the view that customers needed the best facilities that modern life could offer. At the turn of the millennium, the firm had moved from a back-street city-centre building to a purpose-built complex on the city boundary, comprising four different auction rooms, and a further ten exhibition rooms. Inquisitive members of the public could come and browse for free through the thousands of items 'for upcoming auction'. No visit, though, would be complete without allowing the children half an hour in the definitely not free soft play area, or coffee and eye-waveringly expensive cake in the tearoom. Lambert's was also aware of the need for the little things of life: it was the first to offer internet access for free, and large wall-sized television screens broadcast the BBC News Channel all day.

Mary Madeleine Scarlett Maxwell-Hume was banned from Lambert's.

Mary Maxwell-Hume was taller-than-average, yet she could appear quite small. She was slim, yet she could appear overweight. She was bleach-blonde, brunette, grey- and silver-haired, and her hair was both long and short. She never wore the same dress twice in the same month. No one could quite put an age on her. In other words, no one at Lambert's actually had a clue what Mary Maxwell-Hume looked like for sure.

Mary's preferred attire was, shall we say... well-fitted.

Whenever she could, she chose a dress that emphasised her real figure, which was quite tall and fairly slim. She claimed to be a member of the Sisters of Mary of the Sacred Cross, an obscure order whose exact membership numbers were even more obscure; indeed, no one could ever remember seeing two Sisters together in the same location. Sometimes Sisters could be seen out in their striking red nun's habit, but it was never easy to identify which Sister was which. They maintained a website which revealed few details other than the order's motto – in French, not Latin, *Au Naturel, Mon Dieu* – and its core philosophies. The philosophies were mostly unexceptional, bar one: sisters were expected to wear 'only as much clothing as is necessary to provide due modesty'. Sometimes, Mary Maxwell-Hume's choice of dress made it all too clear that she obeyed the Order's rules to the letter.

Mary had one weakness – perhaps all the Sisters had the same weakness – she could never bring herself to meet another human soul without a discreet dab of Chanel No.5 on her wrists and behind her ears. Sometimes not so discreet. Lambert's Auction House might not be able to work out which of the women (or sometimes even men) present was Mary, but they were aware from her scent that she was there somewhere.

Mary knew that, and worked within her limitations, sometimes even using those limitations to her advantage. Once, she managed to panic an auctioneer into knocking down a collection of letters which had survived the *Titanic* disaster at less than a third of the guide price. On another occasion she succeeded in persuading two American golf collectors to bid against each other for a rare nineteenth-century golf ball which would later prove to be a complete fake. She could, and did, cause chaos. She was too clever to bid herself – that would simply have seen her identified and banned in yet another form.

Instead, Mary had *friends*. No one quite knew what hold she had over these men: there was speculation that it might have been blackmail, but readers will be relieved to know that Mary Maxwell-Hume was a woman of strict morals and would never stoop so low. Instead, she selected some of society's unfortunates – lonely divorcees, those recently made redundant, some struggling to provide for families, men with depression and other mental health problems; ex-convicts were particularly well-represented. Mary sought to redress some of life's ills by giving these men's lives some purpose and incidentally redirecting some income in their direction. Redirecting some in Mary's, too, of course.

Mary's 'friends' were detailed off to 'work' Lambert's on her behalf. Sometimes the salesroom was auctioning furniture; on another occasion it might be works of art; or perhaps the sale that day had a music theme – cellos, violins and the like. Indeed it was a music sale that led to Lambert's very first attempt to ban Mary Maxwell-Hume.

Most people have heard of J. S. Bach, in the eyes of many the greatest composer who ever lived. He produced a vast body of work, and towards the end of his life started work on a project called *The Art Of Fugue*. It's not an easy piece. Effectively, there's only the one tune, reworked over and over again, possibly for different instruments, but no one has ever been absolutely sure what Bach had in mind for *The Art Of Fugue*. Some people might regard *The Art Of Fugue* as the most tedious piece of music ever written, but for purists it's intriguing, weaving magical patterns around the listener's ear. What's more, arguably its most fascinating feature is that it was Bach's final masterpiece – literally so, in the sense that he died in the middle of writing it. It's unfinished. Indeed, performances and recordings frequently stop slap bang in the middle of the eighteenth piece, leaving the untrained listener wondering if something's gone wrong; meanwhile the cognoscenti smugly enjoy the opportunity to show off their knowledge by bursting into loud applause.

Needless to say, such a curious piece attracts curious collectors. Ever since Bach's death, ambitious composers have attempted to complete the canon in the great man's style: faintly amusing heard once, but usually fit to be filed away somewhere in a drawer afterwards for ever. And inevitably, there have been rumours of a completed version, written in Bach's own hand and therefore all the more priceless. Perhaps it's in a private collection somewhere? Perhaps something assumed to be the work of a contemporary of Bach's – his son Carl Philipp Emanuel being the chief suspect – was actually the undiscovered Holy Grail?

But the sudden, magical appearance of anything claiming to be a 'complete' version of the unfinished eighteenth *Contrapunctus 18* was always going to be greeted with suspicion by the experts. Had the missing manuscript been claimed as such by its owner, that would indeed surely have been the case. But that wasn't how it happened.

Founded in Leipzig, the Sisters of Mary of the Sacred Cross were a little-known order dating back to the time of the time of Martin Luther. According to its website, the nuns had attempted to bring peace and harmony to the Reformation-era Church by trying to see good in both sides, and had naturally ended up being persecuted by both instead. But instead of bowing to persecution, the Sisters decided to follow the lead of Our Lord and embrace suffering, even choosing the colour red for their habits: blood doesn't show (much) on red clothing. That, though, was all they allowed themselves to wear. If Christ himself was naked on the Cross, then the Sisters surely needed no clothing other than that which was necessary for due modesty. The red habit would suffice.

Nowadays, the Sisters of Mary of the Sacred Cross are an order on the verge of extinction, driven to find peace and calm in the most distant corners of Europe. One such 'distant corner' is the Trinity area of Edinburgh, where the residence of Mary Maxwell-Hume is to be found.

Mary had been giving a piano lesson – giving lessons was her main source of income – to a young woman called Laura who was herself a viola teacher, but who needed to maintain her piano accompaniment skills. As usual, Mary had invited Laura to play some of the accompaniments she had recently found challenging. Then, also as usual, she had finished the session by inviting Laura to rummage around in her copious files of music comprising some little-known pieces by famous composers, some new pieces written by Mary herself, and plenty of 'scraps' – assorted hand-written pieces, usually unsigned. For a change, Laura had dug down, right to the foot of the 'orange box', and emerged with a very old, yellowed piece of paper covered in handwritten, but clear enough, keyboard music. Mary shrugged her shoulders as if to say 'No idea, never seen it before', so Laura set it on the music stand and started to take it on.

Two things were immediately evident. First of all, the piece was completely unplayable. Secondly, the music was familiar: whoever had written it had borrowed Bach's *Art of Fugue* and reworked it. It bore a signature of sorts, but neither Laura nor Mary could make anything of it. The music finished on a bar which progressed Bb, A, C, B.

Intrigued – and rather against Mary's advice – Laura had burrowed down again into the box and found several other old pieces of music. Several were clearly of 18th century origin: for instance there was a collection of tunes by the great Scottish composer and fiddle player Niel Gow. But this solitary fragment intrigued her. What was it? Who had written it?

Mary suggested that Laura take it to an auction house if she were that interested – Lambert's, she suggested, were the most reliable. The pile of musical scraps had been in the Sisters' hands since long before anyone could remember, although Mary Maxwell-Hume herself had attempted to sort out some of them. She recalled some letters on the same type of paper; some were in Latin, some perhaps in Germanic script, but none were in English. She'd passed the letters over to a friend years ago, and had never given any further thought to them. Laura spoke German, and wished she'd had the chance to see them for herself.

Theodore Plews, Director of Lambert's Auction House (Edinburgh) Ltd., took one look at Laura's scrap of paper and suggested it might be 'a minor fragment related to the Niel Gow collection' that Mary Maxwell-Hume possessed, but decreed it to be of 'little interest' otherwise. But at that very moment a passer-by overheard the conversation, older, perhaps, probably around seventy. He asked to have a look at Laura's 'scrap of paper' and wasn't quite so dismissive.

'It's always worth having a quick look at the paper and ink used in anything like this. Check for watermarks and so on, too.' He held it up to the window, studied it, then pronounced, 'Hmm. Where did you say you found this?'

'My piano teacher had it in a box of other bits and pieces,' Laura said. 'I was telling Mr Plews – beside the Niel Gow fiddle pieces and a couple of handwritten fragments on old paper. This one seemed complete – and I recognised a part of the tune.'

Plews was definitely a little put out by this man's interference.

'And you are…?'

'I'm sorry, I should have introduced myself,' the man began, but Laura interrupted him and he wasn't allowed to finish.

'Actually – I've just realised – aren't you Donald Rattray? The famous Perthshire fiddler?'

The man chuckled. 'And there was me thinking I was incognito,' he said. 'But I wouldn't have thought too many people would recognise me, all the same. Are you a musician, too?'

Laura blushed. 'Well, I play the viola a little. Violin, too, of course,' she said. 'I'm only a teacher, though.' She went on to explain that her contact with Mary Maxwell-Hume was because her accompaniment skills needed brushing up.'

'We all owe our careers to a good fiddle teacher or two, Miss…'

Laura introduced herself in return, saying how proud she was to meet the great Donald Rattray of Dunkeld.

'And you'll understand that it was the Dunkeld connection that caught my attention, Laura,' said Rattray. 'As you might know – '

'Of course! Niel Gow came from Dunkeld, too,' said Laura. Meanwhile Plews was watching this conversation go backwards and forwards as though it were a tennis match.

Rattray nodded to acknowledge the compliment. 'Mr Gow was truly a *great* man, Laura. But I'm a student of classical music, too. I'm as happy giving Bach recitals as I am playing at a ceilidh. And did you know that the two great men actually met?'

'They did?' said Laura and Plews, simultaneously.

'Yes indeed,' said Rattray. 'They were contemporaries, you know – so many of these great composers knew each other. Did you know that Bach, Handel and Domenico Scarlatti were born in the same year?'

'Really?' said Laura, wide-eyed.

'I thought everyone knew that,' Plews said dismissively. Laura blushed slightly again, rather humiliated by the unpleasant dapper little man with the Hitler moustache.

'Sorry,' she said. 'Out of interest, what year was that, Mr Plews?'

Plews had over-reached himself: he'd no idea. He pretended he hadn't hear.

'1685, Laura,' Rattray called out. 'I'm not sure Mr Plews actually heard you.'

'I'm sorry, Mr Rattray,' Plews said, 'but my mind was on rather more important matters than a Trivial Pursuit question. I'm a busy man.'

'Of course, of course. I understand,' Rattray said. 'And I quite understand that this discovery is far too big, too historically important, for a small provincial auction house like this to handle. This is for the major league players down in London. I might let King and Castle see it first, perhaps.' King and Castle were Lambert's main competitors in Edinburgh, although Lambert's thought they were a cut above.

'Look, on second thoughts…,' said Plews.

'No, no, you're busy. I appreciate that you personally might not have the confidence or experience to deal with this.'

Plews regrouped and returned to sneer mode.

'If you're the expert, why don't you tell us what you know, Mr Rattray?'

'The theme is definitely *The Art Of Fugue*, Bach's final masterpiece,' said Rattray, 'and the paper might actually be 18th century German. Of course, it could be any 18th century bit of German music, and it could also be someone *pretending* to be Bach, but then there's the music itself.'

'What about the music?' asked Plews, already more than a little irritated with himself that he'd allowed the specialist to usurp his position.

'Well it's obvious, isn't it?' Rattray said. It wasn't, of course, not to anyone else but himself. Seeing the blank looks on the other two faces, he went on, 'It's the final bar – Bb – A – C – B. The B natural in German notation at the time would have been an 'H'. It's like a signature.'

'Bach,' Plews repeated. 'But anyone could have written that.'

'Indeed they could,' the music expert acknowledged. 'What makes it interesting is what it might be, not what it probably isn't.'

Plews often struggled to understand what experts said, but Laura was a little confused, too.

'Could you just explain that?' she said.

'Sorry,' Rattray said. 'I quite understand, it's probably nothing at all. However, although I see lots of old fiddle manuscripts, this one is a little special. This is definitely Niel Gow's handwriting – he had a unique way of setting out the notes. But, it's on an extraordinary kind of paper.' He held it up to the light. 'Can you see that swirling marks at the bottom left…? Those are the marks of handmade paper, made from rags rather than wood fibre. This paper is definitely pre-1800 in date. Paper-makers made their wares from whatever rags were to hand locally, and this is, I'm pretty sure, Eastern European – Polish, perhaps, or more likely Prussian.'

'Is Leipzig a possibility?' Laura asked.

'Leipzig? Why, of course, but why did you ask?'

Laura explained that her piano teacher had inherited some ancient possessions from the city.

'But that's astonishing!' Rattray said. 'That's a real connection.'

'I'm sorry to sound so stupid,' Laura said, 'but your story about Niel Gow and Bach. How would they have met? How would they have even spoken to each other?'

Plews, for his part, wondered this, too, but was glad to have Laura ask the daft questions on his behalf.

'Ah,' said Rattray. 'Now that's an interesting question, and the answer is an extraordinary coming-together of a number of events. Bach died in 1750, just four years after Bonnie Prince Charlie's Jacobite Rebellion ended at Culloden. Niel Gow's great patron in Dunkeld was the Duke of Atholl, who helped defeat the Jacobites by raising troops in Dunkeld itself. As a reward, George II sent the Duke and his favourite musician Gow to meet Bach – and as a translator, sent Handel.'

'They were all there together!' Laura said.

'So the story goes. Handel was bi-lingual by this stage, of course, although legend has it that only the Duke of Atholl could understand Gow.' Laura chuckled as Rattray continued, 'Bach, Handel and Gow played to each other on their preferred instruments – Gow could really only play the fiddle, but he was very good. Anyway, I think this was around 1748, shortly before Bach died and during the very period when he was obsessed with *The Art of Fugue*. It all fits.'

'But it's just a story,' Plews reminded him. 'There's no evidence of any meeting at all, is there?'

Rattray stood silently to allow Plews to consider what he'd just said.

'There *was* no evidence, no. Until now,' he said, eventually. 'But that's just my opinion. You're entitled to yours. Why don't you check it out?'

'I'm not sure who to ask,' Plews admitted.

'How about one of the other auction houses?'

'No!' Plews said, abruptly. 'They'll just try to question it.'

'So what do I do?' Laura asked.

Plews said that there was a Lambert's music sale due the following month. He could include it as a lot for sale if Laura was willing to part with it. Laura said she would check with her piano teacher, but thought it should be fine. Plews agreed to advertise it in the sale with all of the details as supplied by Rattray but thereafter 'sold as yet unauthenticated'.

Theodore Plews knew that written evidence of a meeting involving Bach and Gow would be worth tens of thousands of pounds, perhaps more. He'd already worked out that it was well worth the gamble on spending a couple of hundred pounds to claim ownership now. Of course, he wasn't allowed to bid for the lot himself, that simply wasn't professional. However, Plews had a plan: his cousin Arthur – who conveniently looked nothing like him and was always looking for a way to earn a quick penny – could stand in for him instead.

In the weeks leading up to the music sale, Plews had managed to work himself into quite a frenzy, increasingly certain that this small fragment of paper in a glass case was in fact a priceless link between two utterly divergent cultures. In his own mind, each week added another million to its value.

Arthur was instructed that he was to make sure that he outbid anyone else, up to and including £10,000. Arthur was surprised, but Theodore assured him that if the bidding started to go crazy, then that in itself was reassuring that the document was indeed priceless. Arthur meanwhile made a mental note that cousin Theodore was clearly well-enough off to be tapped for a loan at some point in the future, but in the meantime was to receive £300 for his services at the sale.

By the day of the auction, the musical fragment had received a fair amount of publicity in the local news, as well as in some trade publications. Everyone was aware that buying it was a gamble, but Lambert's had a reputation and Plews was repeatedly quoted saying that the auction house was rarely taken in.

The sale-room was very full by the time Lot 198 came round. He recognised the usual mix: genuine buyers, interested spectators, even some journalists. Plews' eye was drawn to a tallish woman in her early thirties. Dressed in a back-trimmed well-fitting knee-length red dress, she had prominent front teeth, wore bottle-thick glasses, wore her long blonde hair tied back quite severely and was writing notes on a clipboard. She seemed faintly familiar – he was sure she'd covered a Lambert's auction before for a local newspaper. Plews was nervous: he began to worry that even £10,000 might not land his prize. The bidding began briskly, led mainly by two competing men who were standing quite close to each other. Plews himself had taken up his usual position in the middle of the salesroom floor along with the bidders. His eyes darted from side to side, and as the bidding picked up he was pleased to see that Arthur had now entered at just over £1,200. Soon, the price was almost £5,000, and it was around then that he was aware of the tall blonde behind him. To be more exact, he was aware of her Chanel No.5 perfume.

'I'm so glad you find my little scrap of paper intriguing, Mr Plews,' the woman said, adding, 'I do hope you win the auction. It might be a little… difficult if someone else were to discover what you're up to here.'

Plews turned round in horror, but the red-dressed woman was already making her way towards the exit. His nemesis had somehow managed to get into Lambert's undetected, and now she was going to escape, too. Not that there was much he could do, anyway. Plews realised that he was trapped; he'd been duped, but above all he had to stop anyone finding out. He knew that the only route out was to ensure that he himself became the owner of the 'little scrap of paper'.

Turning to Arthur instead, he whispered in his cousin's ear, 'Make sure you win the bid. No matter what.' Arthur raised his eyebrows to say 'you're sure?', but Plews nodded his head vigorously.

In the event, Arthur – well, Plews – had to pay almost £11,000 for a scrap of paper he knew to be worthless. Plus £300 for Arthur's services. But at least he'd preserved his reputation, and Lambert's itself would never find out that he'd broken the company's rules.

∗

Laura and Donald Rattray sat in Whigham's wine bar. Three other adult pupils from Mary Maxwell-Hume's piano-teaching stable had joined them, each of whom been bidding for Mary's 'scrap of paper'. Mary herself was due, but always made a grand entrance precisely five minutes after the official meeting time.

Sure enough, at 7.35, a stunning silver-haired woman in her early fifties glided into the bar. Gone was the red-and-black knee-length skirt, gone were the prominent false front teeth, gone were the blonde wig and bottle-thick glasses. Instead she was dressed in her preferred calf-length *extremely* well-fitted dress – black on this occasion. Only the Chanel No.5 remained.

There was almost £11,000 to divide up. As the major players, Laura and Donald each received £3,000, a recognition, too, that their teenage daughter needed expensive dental treatment not available on the NHS. The three bidders received £1,000 for their work, leaving the remainder, around £1,500 for Sister Mary herself – or as she put it, for necessary expenses.

The group were well onto their second bottle of chardonnay when Donald finally asked the question they all wanted to know.

'Why are we meeting here, Sister Mary? Whigham's isn't your usual haunt.'

Sister Mary smiled quietly. 'Wait, Donald. Wait and see.'

They only had to wait another twenty minutes for their answer. Just before half past eight, Theodore Plews and his wife – who was several inches taller than him, incidentally – entered Whigham's, although they didn't see Mary or her friends.

Mary allowed them to settle into a quiet corner, order a bottle of red wine, then wandered across with another bottle herself and placed it on the table.

'Good evening, Mr Plews. This is on me,' she said. Plews looked furious, but his wife said, 'Good evening, and thank you, Mrs… Aren't you going to introduce us, Teddy?'

Mary took the lead herself. 'My name's Mary Maxwell-Hume. I'm a sort of working acquaintance of… Teddy's,' she said. 'I'm interested in the arts myself.'

'Oh, nice to meet you, Mary. I'm Nancy, Teddy's wife. So what do you do? Are you a collector?'

'No, no,' Mary laughed. 'I'm a piano teacher, really. But I'm actually a nun.'

'A nun! But you're not dressed…'

'I belong to the Sisters of Mary of the Sacred Cross,' Mary said. 'One of our rules is that we only wear as much as is necessary to maintain due modesty.'

She watched as Nancy and Plews absorbed what she'd just said. She was just as amused to watch as Nancy's eyes turned to her husband's, who was glued to Mary's dress. Then Mary leaned over and whispered in Plews' ear – lingering a little longer to allow him to be even more embarrassed by her proximity – 'Mr Plews, you can't cheat an honest man. I hope my music gives you consolation.'

Then she stood upright to go, saying, 'Nice to meet you, Nancy.'

Nancy Plews smiled in return. She quite liked seeing her overbearing husband occasionally silenced. 'Nice to meet you, too, Mary. And by the way I love your perfume. Is that Chanel No.5 by any chance?'

'Well done, Nancy, right first time.'

MARY MAXWELL-HUME AND ME

I first met Mary Maxwell-Hume one July day, three years ago. I'd been called to deal with an incident where she was alleged to have taken a taxi and then refused, or at least failed, to pay the fare. It was a swelteringly hot afternoon, the taxi-driver's temper was a little frayed, and even I was in no hurry to leave my patrol car for the direct glare of the sun as I arrived at the scene.

Curiously enough, the taxi's passenger appeared serenely cool, even in the searing heat. But I'm bound to confess that I really wasn't too concerned about her temperature. Instead I was simply dazzled by her appearance: she was wearing a scarlet red crepe nun's habit that clung to, and accentuated, every last aspect of her body. *Every last part.* Only her head was covered more than might have been expected, for the female passenger was wearing a matching red wimple and red wide-brimmed hat. I'd never seen anything like it, I couldn't take my eyes off her, and I could feel my heart rate soaring just being near.

She wasn't due the driver a lot of money, it transpired, no more than £8.00. However she was determined that the cabbie would leave empty-handed. Her reasoning was that the taxi-driver had taken anything but the most direct route, thus not only running up needless extra money on the meter, but also – and this was the crux of Ms Maxwell-Hume's argument – wasting her time needlessly. She had already made out a handwritten invoice to the driver for her time, and charged at £40 per hour she was attempting to say that it was she, Mary Maxwell-Hume, who should be receiving payment rather than the taxi-driver. The argument had then escalated to the point where he'd locked her into the passenger cabin and called for police assistance. The 'police assistance' that particular day turned out to be me.

Police Scotland had recently taken delivery of a small consignment of those little Smart cars that are really little cubes on wheels and therefore very easy to park. They were really designed to carry just a driver, perhaps with one other passenger in the front seat as well, but they weren't intended as meat-wagons for transporting arrested prisoners back to a police station. As an Edinburgh police constable newly assigned one of these little vehicles, my job was to head quickly to the scene of the incident and to assess first-hand what, if any, further action might be needed. I was to keep in radio contact at all times with headquarters, reporting back what I saw; if possible I was to resolve any issues on the spot. Allocating just one officer to each car in this way had the effect of spreading on-the-beat forces even more thinly than they already were: cars were cheaper than salaried staff.

I remember that I managed to get to the scene of the altercation within three minutes of it being called in. The driver was sitting fuming in his cab, Mary was sitting in the back seat, looking slightly irritated but nevertheless cool and calm. We get called to deal with a few of these incidents each year, and as usual I went over to hear the cabbie's side of things first. Almost invariably the problem is a drunk, threatening or obnoxious fare, although a quick glance into the back suggested that this might not turn out to be a 'usual' incident. As normal, I took a note of the driver's details, which aside from everything else gives him a chance to cool down a little and gather his thoughts. As a result, he began his account with a more considered statement.

'I hate nuns. All of them. Nothing but trouble.'

I took a deep breath. 'Do you want me to note that down, sir?'

'No, suppose not,' he said, grudgingly. 'But I hate nuns.'

Deciding that it might be better to start my report with 'Taxi driver claimed to hate nuns' after all, I typed a few details into my handheld electronic notebook. It seemed that the cabbie had attended Roman Catholic schools and had experienced unpleasant treatment at the hands of those few nuns and priests who taught him. Now, he had it in for everyone in clerical garb. Other than that, his angle was a simple one: she was trying to dodge paying her dues. I asked him to wait for me in his taxi.

I decided to interview the scarlet nun in the panda car as the most private place available and safe from the taxi driver's vitriol. I was *aware* of something about her as we made our way across the road, but once we were each in the tight confines of my Smart car I realised that she was wearing some kind of perfume: recognisable, expensive, subtle yet lasting. Just possibly Chanel No.5.

She must have noticed my unease.

'Are you feeling all right, Constable? It's a very warm day, I feel a little overdressed myself,' and with that she removed both her hat and wimple to reveal a somewhat different person to the one I'd imagined. Mary Maxwell-Hume might be a nun, but she clearly took care with her appearance. Her silver and black hair was neatly and professionally cut. It even, perhaps, sported some sort of gel to make it spiked on top – which she now ran her hands through, having removed her headgear.

Now I had a very close-up view of the red 'habit' she was wearing. Although it was ankle-length, and really didn't reveal much flesh, the material itself clung to her in such a way that absolutely nothing was left to the imagination.

Nothing at all. The material simply stretched itself over and around her form. I was spellbound.

She didn't look at me, although it must have been obvious that I was very much looking at her. Instead, gazing into the distance, she simply said, 'Perhaps we should begin, Constable? Perhaps you'd like to start by giving me your full name?'

More than a little confused, I said, 'I think I'm supposed to ask you that.'

'That's one possibility,' she said. 'But your mind seemed to be on other things so I thought I'd start the conversation. What is your name?'

'PC 1206,' I replied.

'*Really?*' she said. 'Is that what your mother calls you?'

'No... but it's all I'm supposed to give out to the general public.'

'Come now, PC 1206. I'm hardly 'the general public', am I now?'

I couldn't see how it would do any harm, so I told her that my name was PC John Knox. She immediately turned round to face me with a wide smile.

'My, my... John Knox? Really?'

'I think I might be a different 'John Knox', madam,' I muttered. 'Now, what's your full name, please?'

'Sister Mary Madeleine Scarlett Maxwell-Hume. You may address me as Sister Mary if you wish.' Then she added slowly, 'I'm so thrilled to meet John Knox at last.'

'As I said, madam... Sister Mary, I'm not *that* John Knox.'

'Ah yes, but you don't know which John Knox I was looking forward to meeting, do you? I'm delighted to meet you, young man.'

Utterly confused, I decided to ignore her and get on with the job in hand.

'Address?'

'My temporary address, or my permanent one?'

I was struggling to keep calm.

'Let's go for the permanent address, shall we?'

'The Kingdom of God,' she said. 'I'm afraid I don't know the postcode.'

I took a number of deep breaths. 'OK, how about a temporary residence?'

Sister Mary gave me an address in the Trinity area on Edinburgh's north side.

'Date of birth?'

She arched an eyebrow at me. 'Are you asking a woman her age, John?'

'It's just standard procedure, Sister.' Then I added, 'Please?'

She smiled, then gave me a date.

'That's today,' I said, trying to soften things a little more. 'Happy Birthday.'

'Thank you, John.'

'You don't look 53, Sister Mary, if you don't mind me saying so. You'd pass for a woman ten years younger.'

She looked at me carefully. 'I think that's meant as a compliment, young man. Thank you, again.'

I took another deep breath. 'Occupation? I mean, do nuns have occupations like the rest of us?'

'Of course. Or we'd starve to death. Piano teacher.'

I wrote that down, then let her tell me her side of the story. She'd called a taxi to take her into town, and her version was that the driver had taken a ridiculously long route which had been intended to waste both her time and money. She was determined not to pay him.

In the meantime, however, she realised that she'd left her bag, including her purse, at home. She had no means of paying anyway. The cabbie was sure that he'd seen her secrete cash and a credit card inside her habit. That habit.

'Tell me, John, do you think I have anything hidden under my dress? Please tell me? I'll get out of your car and you can study me carefully.'

'No, no,' I said, starting to panic. I was in a predicament. I was sure that Sister Mary was playing me for all I was worth. I tried to delay things by collecting some more useless information.

'What order do you belong to, Sister Mary? I've never seen the red habit before.'

'That's a very perceptive question, John. My order is the Sisters of Mary of the Sacred Cross. If we wear habits, we wear red, although we often wear ordinary clothes as well.'

I wanted to ask her a delicate question, but didn't have the courage.

'I'll help you out.' How did she know? 'Our order believes that we should wear only as much as is necessary to preserve due modesty. In general, clothing is an adornment which glorifies the human body rather than the Lord.'

I tried to take that in. 'You appear to dress... well enough to me.'

'Thank you,' Sister Mary said. 'One must maintain standards.'

Realising that I was becoming completely distracted, I tried to move on.

'Where were you going in the taxi, Sister Mary?'

'The Queen's Hall, just round the corner. My piano pupils are giving recitals there this evening. I forgot to sign a form and I was taking a taxi there and back. I'll only be seconds.'

'A concert tonight? Are your pupils good, then?'

'No, they're awful, actually. Every one of them. They need the harrowing experience of a disastrous concert to bring home just how much work they still have to do.'

Fortunately, I wasn't considering piano lessons myself.

'You say you have no money on your person, Sister Mary.'

'Do you doubt me? Do you want to check? I really don't mind, you know, although I'd rather go somewhere more private.'

It was around about this point that I began to realise that I was totally out of my depth with Sister Mary Maxwell-Hume. No question seemed safe.

'No, Sister Mary, I'd rather take your word for it.'

'Are you sure? It's no trouble.'

'Let's move on, Sister Mary. This taxi driver needs to be paid.'

'If he waits, I could pay him after the return journey.'

'I suspect he's not keen on that plan. A fare in the hand is worth two in the bush.' I realised my mistake as soon as I'd said it. Sister Mary once again offered to let me check to see if she had hidden funds, and I could feel my face reddening. Instead, a faint smile slowly played across her lips.

'The Lord will provide, John. The Lord will provide.'

I got out of my patrol car and wandered over to the taxi driver who by now was really impatient. Opening my own wallet, I gave the cabbie a ten-pound note and asked him to leave me to deal with Sister Mary. He looked a little askance at me and started a few 'I hate nuns' mutterings, but eventually I got rid of him, feeling I'd done my good deed for the day.

When I returned to my patrol car, Sister Mary was still sitting in the passenger seat.

'Have you finished with me yet, Constable?'

'I have, although I need to give you an incident note. It prints from the handheld.'

'It prints from the handheld?' she repeated. 'My, whatever

next?' she added as I handed over the admittedly fairly pointless little ticket. Then a thought occurred to me.

'You said you're popping into the Queen's Hall for a moment. How do you propose to get home?'

Sister Mary looked stoically away from me out of the passenger-side window.

'Well, I suppose I'll have to walk, won't I, Constable?'

I sighed. 'If you're back here in two minutes I'll run you home.'

Mary gave me her widest smile yet. 'Why, Constable, how Christian of you! That would be very kind.'

I ignored her attempts to butter me up. 'If you're not back in three minutes – 180 seconds, mind you – I'll not be here. Go!'

Sure enough, four minutes later we were on our way back to Trinity, although I confess to having a little fun by pretending not to see her coming and setting off slowly up the road. Briefly, very briefly, I saw her break into a slightly panicked trot which gave me an equally brief and mischievous sense of power.

'Bad boy, Constable Knox,' she said as she eventually made it into the seat.

I didn't rise to her admonition, but instead drove in complete silence until we were well past the city centre and heading north towards the suburbs. Then, slightly unexpectedly, an other incident was called in: the incidents weren't unusual, you'll understand, but Sister Mary had rather made me forget that in general I was supposed to be a patrolling police officer.

The owner of a newsagent in the middle of Granton Road had phoned in to say that three youths had barged into his shop and simply filled their pockets with crisps and snacks, chocolate and drinks and run straight out again. I hadn't a choice, I had to go straight there. We were close to the newsagent's shop when Sister Mary surprised me by producing a mobile phone from somewhere – I'm not sure where she could have concealed it in her dress without it being totally obvious, but that's another matter – and started taking photographs as we went along the street.

Arriving at the newsagent's shop, I recognised an old community friend, Mr Ahmed, behind the counter. He was both angry and resigned at the same time: this sort of thing happened almost every other week. He'd seen the boys in the shop before. Sometimes there was a girl with them, but not this time. No, he couldn't put names to them, but they were from the local secondary school.

I knew there was little I could do. I could hardly stop all the kids in the local area and ask them to empty their pockets; nor could I go into the school and throw my weight about – schools are sensitive about that sort of thing. All I could perhaps do would be to speak to the local headmaster and ask him to say something at an assembly. Mr Ahmed looked at me sadly. He knew my hands were tied.

I've no idea what made me look round just then; perhaps it was the Chanel No.5 again. Anyway, there she was behind me: Mary had got out of my car and followed me in. She said nothing at all, she was simply *there*, present in Mr Ahmed's shop, holding a mobile phone so that Mr Ahmed could see the screen clearly.

'That's them!' he said. 'Those are the very boys! Where did you take that picture?'

I wanted to know the answer to that question myself.

'Round the corner,' Mary said. 'In Afton Terrace.'

'But why…? How?' I asked. 'How did you know to take *these* boys' picture?'

'Don't you think it's a little odd when a teenage boy has

seven bars of chocolate sticking out of his pocket? And they're all the *same* chocolate bar?'

I knew the two boys' names by heart. One of them, Frankie Moran, was on a last chance before being taken into care. Even I didn't think that was a good idea, and I said so to Sister Mary. Nor did Mr Ahmed. He was a good man. He deserved better than to have his chocolate stolen.

'Why don't we see if we can find them?' Sister Mary said.

'I should be calling for police assistance, Sister Mary. This isn't your job.'

'John,' she said, speaking my name very softly, 'do you want to arrest these children, or do you want to make them better?' She glanced at Mr Ahmed. 'If you arrest these boys, Mr Ahmed will continue to get young people coming into his shop to steal. Isn't it time to try something else?'

I'd no idea what she meant, but Sister Mary is very persuasive. Even Mr Ahmed just shrugged his shoulders.

We got back into the car, and set off in the direction of where they were last seen. In no time at all Mary asked me to stop the patrol car and asked to get out; she said that the boys would be found round the corner down by the park.

Sure enough, I saw the two boys together in Victoria Park. I got out, parked the car, and approached them, whereupon of course they fled. I'd no chance of catching them, though, as they sped off down a quiet side street. Suddenly, though, I heard screams and yells, and as I arrived, I discovered the boys flat on the pavement.

'She tripped me! She tripped us both up!' Frankie yelled. He'd grazed his hand, but was otherwise unhurt. Indeed he'd have got up were it not for the fact that Sister Mary was sitting on top of him. The other boy, Tam Lomond, was too stupid to try to run away, but in any case Sister Mary had tied the laces of his trainers to a fence in a ferocious knot.

'These boys assaulted me,' Mary insisted. 'I'm quite bruised.'

'Bitch!' Frankie said from the ground.

Then Mary did something quite remarkable. She grabbed Frankie by the nose, and yanked his face up from the pavement and round to look at her directly.

'Look,' she said, 'I'm about to make you the best offer you'll ever get. The most important decision of your life. Your choice.'

I wasn't sure I wanted to hear the next bit.

'Choice No. 1: PC Knox arrests you and you end up in care. You *are* Frankie, aren't you?'

'Yes.'

'Choice No. 2: You go back and pay for those bars of chocolate. You're nice to Mr Ahmed, you say sorry, and you offer to make amends. Do you know what that means, Frankie?'

'I think so. But I've no money, Miss.'

'I thought not. Well, I've got an idea. I think nice Mr Ahmed could do with a little help in his shop, don't you? Help him sweep the floors, even help supervise the shop at lunchtime to make sure nobody steals.' She turned to Tam, who was still wrestling with his shoelaces. 'Interested, Tam? Or would you like a criminal record?' She took out her mobile phone and showed the boys the photographs.

Tam panicked slightly. 'Please, Miss. My Dad will kill me.'

'Well, then. Do we have a deal?'

I had to point out that I didn't have room for Mary and the boys.

'PC Knox,' Mary said, 'we have to trust these boys. I know they'll go back to see Mr Ahmed in his shop. But I think we should go on ahead.'

Ten minutes later, the boys appeared in Mr Ahmed's shop again; we were there to greet them. They returned the uneaten bars of chocolate, but they were still due £1.20. Mary had asked Mr Ahmed simply to accept what the boys offered. Even he was taken aback by their offer to sweep the shop and supervise at lunchtimes. He managed to resist saying that they would be well qualified to spot shoplifters. Instead, he actually promised to offer the boys a small payment: after all, if he lost less stock to shoplifters, he, too, would be better off. Faced with a little kindness, even the hardened Frankie was a little moist-eyed. But he was still a teenage boy, that hadn't changed.

'Miss.'

'Yes, Frankie?'

'Can I ask you a question, Miss? A personal question, like?'

Mary smiled. 'Go on, Frankie. Ask what you like. I might not answer.'

Frankie hesitated. 'That's a nice dress.'

'Thank you. It's called a 'habit' actually.'

'Are you wearing anything underneath it?'

Mr Ahmed was horrified. I simply said, 'Frankie!' Mary, however, simply smiled.

'PC Knox, Mr Ahmed, I said Frankie could ask anything at all. I keep my promises. Don't we all?' She gave the boys each a hard look. Then she smiled again.

'What do you think? You can have a good look.'

'Can I?'

'That's what I said.'

'Can I touch?'

'Absolutely not, Frankie. But you can look as long as you like. Would you like me to turn around for you?'

Frankie was spellbound, so Mary turned very slowly

The Discreet Charm of Mary Maxwell-Hume

round, smoothing her dress – sorry, habit – against her body as she did so.

'Well?' she said. 'Satisfied, Frankie?'

Eventually, Frankie managed three words: 'Thank you, Miss.'

'I kept my promise, boys. Will you keep yours?'

'Yes, Miss,' they said in unison, although it was more of a whisper.

Then Mary turned to me. 'Mr Ahmed is out of pocket by £1.20,' she said. 'I'd pay it myself, but unfortunately as you know...'

I got the hint. I dug into my pocket and paid over the money. After the taxi fare, it wasn't so much, really.

'They're just teenage boys, you know, John. You did a wonderful job there,' Mary said on the way back to the patrol car. Of course I was giving her a lift the rest of the way home. 'You stopped a crime from happening, two boys found a little part-time job, and Mr Ahmed will find life a little easier in his shop from now on.'

I chose not to say that she'd been responsible for everything.

'You know,' she went on, 'I wouldn't be surprised if Mr Ahmed gets in touch with the Chief Constable some time this week to say how wonderful you are.'

'I rather doubt that,' I said. We'd reached her house at last.

'Would you like a cup of tea, John? I could give you what I owe you. I'll need to change into something a little lighter first, though. It's quite a warm day.'

I had to laugh. 'No thanks, Sister Mary.'

'Please call me Mary, John. I'd like to think we could be

friends. Although remember that I'm a nun.'

'How could I forget?'

She turned to face me and smiled in that now-familiar quietly enigmatic way. I wondered what was coming. In fact, she simply infused me with herself – I can't describe it any other way – liberally aided and abetted by Chanel No.5, of course.

Five days later, the Chief Constable popped into our local station. He'd had a personal letter from a Mr Ahmed Aziz, a newsagent in Granton Road, praising the way I'd tracked down two young shoplifters, brought them back, and instead of throwing the book at them had persuaded Mr Ahmed to employ them on a part-time basis. He was going to have an article written about me in the internal police newspaper, as an example of community policing at its very best. There was no mention of Sister Mary Maxwell-Hume.

IN THE TUNNEL OF DARKNESS

On Edinburgh's east side lie two areas, Meadowside and Seaview, each of which has a long history of social problems: deprivation, poor housing, poor health and unemployment. Both areas have actually picked up a lot recently, but they've a lot of catching up to do, and although they will eventually settle down eventually as they eventually gentrify, the two suburbs currently take up more than their fair share of police time.

Between the two estates runs a pedestrian tunnel. It's not a place for the faint-hearted, and even locals are wary of The Tunnel. Nobody, especially a woman, would go there alone, certainly not at night, and The Tunnel is generally home to drug addicts, dealers and the local gangs. Sometimes the gangs, addicts and dealers turn out to be all the same people, and the graffiti on its walls bear witness to the ever-changing power struggles between those that inhabit The Tunnel's murky depths. Even the police take care anywhere near The Tunnel in darkness; sometimes it's referred to as 'The Tunnel of Darkness'.

By now, I'd acquired a new friend. Mary Maxwell-Hume was an odd sort of acquaintance for a fresh-faced policeman in his late twenties, but then Mary Maxwell-Hume was an extraordinary sort of woman. I won't deny it: she had me wrapped around her little finger, and at least three or four times each week she had me performing little 'duties' on her behalf. She might ask me to call round to hang a picture up, or put a shelf up. I had to cut her grass in the back garden one day. But by far the most common request was for a lift in my Smart patrol car, which was effectively a two-seated parking machine. I might have to take her to the supermarket, to buy a new dress, or to purchase some new recording of one of her favourite piano pieces from a shop near Edinburgh Castle that specialised in classical music CDs.

All of this taxi-driving naturally had to be fitted in around my duties as a police officer. I'd become quite used to attending incidents with Mary riding shotgun in the passenger seat, but I was taking her home one day when I realised that I'd forgotten to take my evening meal out of the freezer. I explained that I wanted to nip home to my flat and take it out. When we arrived, she surprised me by getting out of the car, too.

'I'd like to see where you live, John. Would you mind?' Mary had long since ceased to address me 'P. C. Knox', 'Officer' or 'Constable'.

I could hardly say no; in any case, I'd been inside *her* house many times. But I knew immediately what would catch her eye as I showed her into my living room.

'My, John! It's a piano! How lovely! You have surprised me.'

'My granny left it to me in her will. I'm afraid I don't play it.'

'Don't you like piano music, John?'

'I do like listening to the piano, Mary. I'm afraid I'm not very musical myself, though.'

She turned to look at me. 'Really? What makes you so sure of that, John?' I should take this opportunity to describe my visitor's appearance. If we start from ground level, Mary was wearing a pair of elegant black leather sandals, and from the ankles upwards she was wearing a black and red striped fine woollen dress which, as ever, accentuated and revealed every last contour of her figure. And that was all, apart from the inevitable dabs of Chanel No.5 which now suffused my patrol car so beautifully. There were two reasons that I knew that she chose to wear only a dress. First of all, she was a nun, and claimed to be a member of the Sisters of Mary of the Sacred Cross, whose rules insisted that its followers wear 'only as much clothing as is required to maintain due modesty'; secondly, I could tell simply by looking. Which I tried not to do any more than I could help. She was twice my age, but she could still distract me.

Eventually, I remembered that I was supposed to be answering a question.

'Sorry, Mary. My mind was elsewhere.'

She smiled quietly, knowingly. 'Why do you think you aren't musical, John?' she repeated. Her voice was softer, but more insistent.

'I actually did some piano lessons as a wee boy, but I wasn't very good.'

'Perhaps your teacher wasn't very good, John.'

'No, Mary, I don't believe you can make silk purses out of sows' ears.'

'John,' she said sharply. 'A good teacher can always teach any pupil anything. Some just take a little longer to learn than others, but they're the more rewarding ones.'

'I think I might take so long that we'd both be dead before I made anything of it,' I said. 'I'm the Mount Everest of piano teaching, I suspect.'

I'd intended it to sound amusing, but it produced an unexpected response.

'John, I'm going to give you piano lessons. For nothing. I'll teach you how to play your piano.'

'That's a kind offer, Mary, but I hardly think it's necessary. Thanks anyway.' Privately, I was thinking, How do I get out of this?

'Really?' she said, archly. 'Hardly necessary? Is your piano playing so good that you don't require tuition.'

'That's not what I meant, Mary.'

'What *did* you mean, then?'

I realised that I'd dug myself into a very deep hole indeed. I didn't want to sound ungrateful and Mary had already proved herself a useful companion once or twice. Hers was a friendship that I wasn't sure I wanted to – could – give up. She was under my skin.

'What did you have in mind in the way of lessons, Mary?'

'It depends how good you are.'

'Bad. I learned piano until I was eleven years old then football took over. Then girls.'

'Do you have a girlfriend just now, John?'

That hurt a little. I sighed. 'Not at the moment.'

'In that case, John, you need a substitute.'

I gently suggested that playing the piano might not meet my needs in the same way as a girlfriend. Especially physically. But I'd underestimated her.

'But that's just where you're wrong, John. The piano is such a *sensuous* instrument. You can massage the keys in the same way as you massage a woman's body.'

'Really?'

'It's excellent practice, John. Honestly.' Suddenly, she became businesslike. 'Look, John, I need to hear what you're like. And I also need to hear what the piano is like. Is it in tune?'

'Amazingly, I had it tuned only last year,' I said, enthusiastically.

Mary looked less than impressed. 'All right. Play me something. Anything. Whatever you played last.'

'That was probably fifteen years ago.'

'I don't believe you, John. When that piano was delivered, you'll have tried to play something. And nobody gets a piano tuner out to a piano then doesn't play it afterwards.'

Once again, she'd cornered me. I was also on duty and keen to get back to work, so reluctantly, I tried out a very heavy-handed version of Satie's *Gymnopédie No. 1*.

'Play it again,' she instructed. 'Play it as though you're massaging the piano.' The she added, 'Play it as though you're massaging me.'

I looked at her, horrified, but she simply looked away, shrugged her shoulders, and asked me to give her a massage – on the piano. I had another go, which she declared was 'much better than the first time.'

'You're better than you make out, John,' she said. Just as I was about to glow with pride, she added, 'but that's still not very good. You need lessons. The piano's better than you are a pianist.'

'That wouldn't be hard,' I pointed out.

'No, it wouldn't,' she said.

After that we settled into a rhythm. Mary gave me piano lessons, I became her personal chauffeur. I was never sure if I was improving or not, but Mary insisted that 'my progress was tangible.' For the most part she gave lessons at her own house, but from time to time she came to my flat, often before I went on night shift. On such occasions, I'd have to go on shift early, take out my Smart patrol car, collect Mary to bring her to my flat on the Southside, then take her home again to Trinity on my way to work.

A couple of months later, we were on our way home quite late one Friday night when I received an emergency call: was anyone in the vicinity of The Tunnel? Whenever Mary was in the car with me I used to pray that no one would call for help, because I was pretty sure that she'd want to be in on the action. I could order her to stay in the car, but I was fairly certain that she'd ignore me, and to be fair, I couldn't really stop her. She'd committed no crime, and as long as she didn't contaminate any evidence or enter the scene of any crime, she could watch from a distance.

The emergency call said that a local dog walker had phoned in to say that two rival gangs were at either end of The Tunnel and were about to attack each other. A dog-walker had spotted a large group of youths heading for one end and, knowing the signs, had immediately dialled 999. All nearby patrol cars were ordered to head for the Meadowside/Seaview pedestrian tunnel immediately. As fate would have it, I was nearby. What I didn't realise was that, being a Friday night, our undermanned force was at full stretch and I was on my own.

I parked the car – slightly concerned to see no signs of any other police cars – and instructed Mary to sit tight in the car. I actually locked her in to give her a little protection against anyone outside who found her in the car, but of course she herself could open the door at any time. Then I ran off down the path to The Tunnel. I could hear the commotion from a couple of hundred yards distance.

When I arrived there, the first thing I realised was that, in the darkness, I couldn't do much – I could flash my torch around but that was about all. Two groups numbering around a dozen each were facing each other about ten or fifteen yards apart, shouting obscenities and threats, and my torch occasionally revealed the glint of a scattering of knives at waist level. In the dark confines of The Tunnel, the noise was magnified, and my shouts to stop went either unheard or ignored. It was just too dangerous to go in on my own – there was every chance I'd get hurt completely accidentally – so I radioed in for emergency police assistance. The control room didn't sound too hopeful that any would arrive soon, but moments later I did receive an order that on no account was I to try to go in on my own.

I'd had to go outside a little to get radio reception, and by the time I'd received the second message ordering me to wait for assistance, there was a new sound in The Tunnel. Or, to be exact, there was no sound.

That's often a sign that someone has been hurt, and thinking of the knives I rushed back to the entrance of The Tunnel to see if there had been a stabbing. Flashing my torch round, I saw a few dazzled faces turn to look at me, but they wouldn't have been able to pick out more than my dark figure silhouetted against the moonlit sky. That might have been my chance to shout out that I was 'the police', but my torch had picked out something quite unexpected altogether.

The gap between the two groups of youths was still there, but now there was a figure standing between them: a woman, slim, silver-haired, perhaps in her fifties, and wearing an extremely neat-fitting deep red dress. The dress seemed to glow in the dark. I shone the torch on her to make sure my eyes weren't deceiving me, which made the dress glow even brighter. A combination of my torch and the reflected light from the dress in her silver hair made the woman appear to have a halo. Perhaps she did.

''Hello, P. C. Knox,' she called over the heads of one of the gangs in my direction. 'It's so good to see you here.'

'Good evening, Sister Mary. You turn up in the least likely of places.'

Several of the youngsters gasped. 'Sister? Are you one of those nuns, then?'

Mary looked round. 'Yes, I'm a nun. And because I come in peace, I know that none of you would dream of harming me. But I'd still like you to put your knives away. You might hurt each other.'

There were one or two girls present, and one young woman said, 'Are you one of those nuns that wears red tight dresses? I've seen you wandering about town.'

'I am.

'Is it true that you don't wear very much?'

'I belong to the Sisters of Mary of the Sacred Cross. Our order believes that we should wear only as much clothing as is necessary to preserve modesty,' Mary explained.

That appeared to take a moment to sink in, but then the girl went on.

'It's a nice dress, Sister. It's very shiny.'

'Thank you.'

'I don't understand, Sister. Are you saying that underneath your dress, I mean…' As she asked the question, it crossed my mind how much young people are allowed to ask about things that adults shy away from.

'We wear only as much clothing as is necessary to preserve modesty,' Mary repeated. 'Is anything showing?'

'No,' the girl said. 'Not really.' If the light had afforded her a better view, she might have had some doubts.

'Then I've answered your question, my dear,' Mary said.

One young man was less than impressed by Mary's dress.

'I think you should get out of the way, Sister. We have business to conduct here.'

'Why should I get out of the way?' Mary asked. 'Your 'business' is just to cause harm to others, isn't it?'

The boy's jaw jutted out a little more. 'My business is my business alone. It's none of yours.'

Mary looked at him; my torch remained on her, like a spotlight on centre stage.

'Perhaps,' she said. 'But it looks as though, so long as I stay in the way, you'll not be able to do that harm. Or at least, you'll have to get past me to do it.'

'That's not so hard. We can all just barge past you,' he pointed out.

'Suppose I lie on the ground here,' Mary said. 'You'll have to stand on me to get past me.'

'You wouldn't,' said the girl. 'That ground is filthy. Dogs do their business here. People do the toilet. You'd ruin your nice dress.'

Mary paused for a minute.

'Our order doesn't say the dress has to be clean. It just has to cover me.'

'I still don't believe you'd do it,' said the boy. 'You haven't got the guts.'

At that point I knew Mary had won; there was only one outcome. Looking around, she picked a spot: I can't imagine any part of the path through The Tunnel was acceptable at all, but somehow she made a choice. Crouching down, she brushed the ground lightly with her hand, touched a few other parts to check they were dry, and went down on one knee.

'No!' It was the boy who told her to stop. 'You win.'

Mary looked up at him. 'Is it the dress you're worried about, or me?'

The boy hesitated. 'Bit of both.'

'Can I get up?' Mary asked. 'Or are you going to start fighting as soon as I do?'

'No fighting.' He nodded to someone on the other side, who from where I was standing behind seemed to nod as well.

Mary pushed herself up. 'Does anyone have a clean paper handkerchief?' she called out. No one answered, so I stepped forward with one, which she used to wipe her hands. I'd expected her to use it for something else, but she said, 'No,

I'm afraid the dress is ruined.'

Now, finally, it was my turn to speak to the two gangs.

'Look,' I said, 'I could trick you into waiting until my colleagues arrive. They are coming, it's just a busy Friday night. Or I could suggest that each of you leaves The Tunnel the way you came. But you came here to fight, to deal in drugs, and to buy them. You've got money on your person. Sister Mary here has ruined an expensive dress to save you from getting hurt.' I took off my hat. 'OK, everyone, before you leave, I want a nice big contribution towards a replacement.'

I was surprised how meekly they handed over five, ten, even twenty pound notes. Some of the youngsters even said 'Sorry' to Mary as they did so, to which she responded... by blessing them. Once the hat had been round them all, I sent them on their way, but not before the girl had one last question.

'That smell, Miss. Is it your deodorant?'

'No, my dear, that's my Chanel No.5 perfume,' Mary replied. 'Do you like it?'

'Too strong for me,' the girl said.

As they departed, I quietly asked her if the sum we'd collected would cover the cost of her dress.

'Perhaps it would pay for the deposit.'

'Sorry,' I said. 'But thanks for your help.'

'Don't worry about the dress, John. I do have one or two others at home.' I didn't doubt that. ' And it went in a good cause, I'd suggest.'

'Until next Friday.' Three more police cars had arrived simultaneously, too late for the action as usual. I decided that the best course of action would be to say that the two gangs had fled when they'd heard that lots of police were on their way. Involving Mary Maxwell-Hume in the incident could only complicate things.

I still had to take Mary home to Trinity. In the car, I noticed that the Chanel No.5 was even stronger than usual.

'Your perfume had them interested, Mary,' I said.

'It's not for young people. And it's very expensive.'

'It's stronger than usual. Is there a reason?' I wondered if perhaps it worked in tandem with a woman's natural scent.

'Of course,' she said. 'You didn't think I was going to take on thirty sweaty youths in a dark tunnel without something to help, did you? I added some more before I left the car.'

I thought about that for a moment.

'But... forgive me, Mary, but where do you keep the bottle? There's hardly anywhere on your dress to hide it, is there?'

'Are you sure?' she asked. That mischievous smile was back, but she was looking out of the passenger window away from me. 'Do you want to search me?'

We'd stopped at the lights, thankfully. I couldn't help but glance briefly again at the dress.

'No, I don't want to search you, but my casual glance says there's no bottle of perfume hidden underneath your dress.'

Her face was still turned away from me, teasing me.

'Some detective you are, John.'

'I'm not a detective, but go on.'

'I have a small container stuffed down the passenger seat of this car.' She held up a tiny black and gold atomiser, roughly the size of a cigarette lighter, and shook it in my direction. 'It's there all the time. I hope you don't mind.'

I laughed. 'You're a woman of many surprises, Mary.'

Finally, she turned to face me. 'Oh, I do hope so, John. I do hope so.'

THE RELUCTANT HERO

When I first knew her, Mary Maxwell-Hume – or Sister Mary Maxwell-Hume of the Sisters of Mary of the Sacred Cross to use her full title – was a well-known figure in the Trinity area of north Edinburgh. No more than that, though. Seen as more than a little eccentric, Mary gave piano lessons to make ends meet, and rumour had it that she charged quite a lot for a service which, she claimed, 'guaranteed success'. And in truth, she was hardly a spendthrift. She owned outright the terraced villa in which she lived, she ate little, and she was a master of... well, getting other people to pay for things one would normally have expected to have been met from her own pocket.

Sister Mary wasn't unknown to the police. There had been some reports that she was involved in a couple of dubious schemes that had relieved some individuals of their money; but there had been no formal complaints at all. The nearest thing to a formal complaint had come from an odious little man called Theodore Plews, the director of the Edinburgh branch of Lambert's Auction House. He was convinced that Mary Maxwell-Hume was conducting some sort of personal vendetta against him, but I couldn't find any real evidence that Mary had ever actually set foot in the building. In any case, each time I interviewed Plews, I left feeling almost sympathetic towards anyone who might be giving the man a hard time.

Mary had also helped us – well, me – once or twice by resolving one or two little local problems: shoplifting, vandalism, gang violence, that sort of thing. More often than not she shouldn't have been at the scene of the crime, but I ended up giving her so many lifts in my little Smart patrol car that she became a bit of a fixture. Invariably, she rewarded me by making sure that I, not she, received all the credit. No beat bobby was better known to the Chief Constable then me. But it was all minor stuff.

That all changed one spring day almost exactly two years ago. Once again, I was giving Mary a lift back to Trinity. We were chatting happily about the weather and piano pupils when suddenly a message came over my radiophone speaker: a bank was being raided in Goldenacre and all nearby cars were instructed to go immediately to the scene.

Given where I was heading, we'd no choice but to divert straight away. Not that much of a 'diversion' was called for, as we were there in just 35 seconds. I ordered Mary at all costs to stay in the car outside and dashed in.

What I hadn't been told was that there was only the one robber, and that the intruder was wearing a balaclava and armed with a Glock semi-automatic pistol. That discovery stopped me abruptly in my tracks, especially when the robber swung round and instinctively pointed the gun at me. Staring – literally – down the barrel of a gun is not a pleasant experience and when he ordered me to get down and lie flat on the floor, I was in no position to debate the matter. There were only two other customers in the bank, and they were in precisely the same position as me. One was an elderly lady who was quietly weeping with terror; the other was a much younger man for whom lying on a very large midriff was causing considerable breathing difficulties.

'Hand it over, hand it over,' the gunman screamed at the teller. She started to explain that it would take a little while to retrieve any available money from tills – I noticed that she didn't mention the safe – but he just screamed louder. It was my first experience of a live armed robbery, but I'd been trained: keep the robber calm. It's when armed robbers start to get agitated and panic that shots get fired. The teller had obviously been trained well, too, because she did everything very slowly and deliberately. On her own at the front of the small branch, one of her colleagues at least would have been at the back. But banks made it absolutely clear to their staff: this was no time for heroics. Indeed some banks actually threatened any member of staff who broke that rule with dismissal.

It seemed to take a lifetime – mine, perhaps? – to fill the small rucksack with whatever the teller could find. I remember realising that this must have been the very same woman who must have pressed the alarm button that had summoned me. What use to her was I lying here, I asked myself? I tried to concentrate on the welfare of the elderly woman who seemed to be in state of shock, and of the obese man and his struggles to breathe. All this time, the agitated armed robber was yelling at the teller that she needed to 'hurry up, but no quick movements!'

Eventually, he was satisfied that the bag was full enough, and he snatched it back from the teller. Turning back to the door, he started to run then stopped suddenly.

Grabbing a sneak peak of what was going on behind me, I saw a truly extraordinary sight silhouetted in the bright doorway. Standing just inside and her back to the bank's closed glass door, was a figure dressed in a red, extremely-well fitting dress; she was blocking the robber's exit. My mind was in such turmoil that it took me a few seconds to process Mary Maxwell-Hume's presence. How had she managed to get in unnoticed? Then, at floor-level, I spotted it: she was barefoot. I actually had time to realise that she'd reduced her entire clothing complement by two-thirds. She'd even had time to place her discarded shoes neatly at the door.

'Get out of the way!' the robber said.

Mary didn't reply.

'Get of the way!' he screamed again.

'You don't really want me to do that,' Mary said. I started to tell her to do as the man said, but she told me to be quiet.

'Who are you, telling me what to do and what not to do?' the robber said. 'I'll shoot. I've no problems with shooting women.'

Mary paused for a moment, then a smile played across her face.

'Yes, but would you shoot a nun?'

'A nun?'

'A nun. I come in peace. And to save you.'

'Eh?'

'You won't shoot me. You're a decent man, there's too much good in you.'

'How do you know that?' he said. 'You've never met me before.'

'There's good in everyone. Even you. Leave the gun and the bag behind and leave.'

'I'm telling you, I'll shoot!' the robber said.

'Do as he says, Sister Mary,' I shouted. 'For crying out loud, it's too dangerous!'

'I don't think he's going to shoot anyone, especially a nun,' Mary said.

'You don't look like a nun,' the intruder said.

'I belong to the Sisters of Mary of the Sacred Cross. We're just like any other sort of nun, except that we dress slightly differently. We believe that we should only wear whatever clothing is necessary to provide due modesty.'

I could see the man taking that in. He studied the dress more carefully.

'Does that mean that… underneath…?'

'Would you like to find out? Is it all right if I come a little closer?'

The robber nodded.

That brought her closer to me as well, and it was then that I noticed something else: Chanel No.5. When Mary was around, it was always in the air, but it was almost as though she'd added a little extra for the occasion.

'Shall I demonstrate?'

The robber stood transfixed as Mary bent down and very, very slowly began to roll her red dress up from her ankles. The dress passed her calves, then her knees, then she began to roll it up her thighs until...

Suddenly, the robber told Mary to stop. He was satisfied, he said.

'You see, I told you there was good in you,' Mary said, letting the dress fall again and smoothing it out. 'You just needed to have it brought out of you. A man like you wouldn't have shot a nun. Even if you had, you couldn't have shot me without giving P. C. Knox there the chance to jump up and disarm you before you left. You'd have to have turned your back on him.' Then she added, 'Would you, Scotty? It is Scotty Livingston, isn't it? I remember giving you piano lessons quite a few years ago. My, this is a fine mess you've got yourself into.'

'How did you...?'

'Why not take that woollen balaclava off, Scotty?'

Meekly, the gunman did as he was told. I was surprised how much younger he looked than I'd expected, barely twenty, if that.

Mary smiled gently. 'I think you need help, don't you, not the contents of that rucksack. And someone like you doesn't need a gun to prove he's a man, either.' She nodded. 'Put it down on the floor. This is your chance to start again.'

Incredibly, he did just that.

'Now give me the rucksack, Scotty.'

Once again, he meekly handed over the rucksack.

Mary turned to me. 'Constable? I think this is where you take over.'

By now I'd scrambled to my feet and suddenly I found myself holding a rucksack, a gun, and for some reason the balaclava, too. It was as though Scotty were under Mary's spell. I'd seen it plenty of times before, even been under her spell myself, but this was different.

'It wasn't loaded anyway,' he said.

'See, Scotty? I knew there was good in you all along.' Mary continued, 'Now, why don't you let P. C. Knox take you and the gun outside and away from here.' Turning to me she said, 'Do you need the rucksack?'

'I'm afraid so,' I said. 'Evidence.' I could see the disappointment in Mary's eyes. I knew her well enough to know that she might have 'charged a commission' for rescuing the bank's money. I think Mary caught me smiling, because she returned a quiet smile of her own, and a slight shrug of the shoulders.

'Why don't you let the Constable take you outside, Scotty?' Mary said softly. 'You won't need handcuffs, will you?' It was addressed to Scotty, but it was an order to me. 'Scotty, I shall pray for you tonight. I'll pray that the judge sees the goodness in you and gives you only a short jail sentence.'

Scotty looked somewhat confused by the thought of being in Mary Maxwell-Hume's thoughts at night. He knew for sure that at night he'd be thinking about Mary, or more particularly that red dress as it rolled up her legs.

'You might get the chance to speak to the judge in person, Sister Mary,' I pointed out. 'As a witness at the trial.'

'Oh, that's good,' she said. 'I shall look forward to it.' I wondered what the judge would make of Sister Mary. 'Now off you go. By the way, John, I'll need a lift home. You can't expect me to walk after all this,' Mary added, slipping her shoes on again. She said it as though I were her chauffeur.

It was only when Scotty and I left the bank that I remembered that a complete armed response unit would have been called. We emerged to a phalanx of bullet-proof-clad men and women, each with guns pointing at the pair of us. I think I was more scared of being shot by mistake then than by Scotty Livingston just a few minutes earlier.

Somehow or other I ended up as the hero, of course. The press managed to take photographs, some bystanders in flats opposite had mobile phone footage, and I was on every front page and TV news broadcast that evening. Naturally, my report featured Mary Maxwell-Hume's role in the events, but no one seemed to believe me: on the contrary, it was held up as evidence of my exceptional modesty. Mary was interviewed and spoke only of my exceptional courage in talking the gunman into giving himself up. I've no idea how she persuaded the others in the bank that day to give the same story.

Anyway, the upshot was that, once again, I was singled out for exceptional and quite unwarranted praise within the force. Of course I was embarrassed, and when I visited her at home a week later, I took the matter up with Mary herself. She was having none of it.

'John,' she said sharply. 'I'm a nun. I'm a Sister of Mary of the Sacred Cross. How would fame sit with a woman in my position?' I didn't reply, so she went on. 'On the other hand, you're a young man at the start of your career. It's difficult for you young people nowadays, and you should be glad of any little assistance I can offer.'

'Oh I am, Mary, I am. Please understand that. But I feel a bit of a fraud – I'm to receive a police commendation for bravery.'

'But you *were* brave, John. You went into that bank not knowing what you would face, and you didn't panic when faced with a gun. Did you see those other customers? They almost died of shock. But not you.'

'And where does that place you, Mary?'

'I had God to protect me.'

I laughed. 'And the dress. And Chanel No.5.'

She smiled. 'Those, too. Now you see how God protects our order.'

I nodded to indicate that I understood, but actually I still didn't.

'You will, John. One day.' She could read my mind? 'Actually, I think you're starting to understand already.' Perhaps she had other special powers.

I tried to absorb all Mary had said, then decided to settle for what I had and changed the subject.

'Tell me, Mary,' I said, 'what do you get out of this? You've not even received any reward.'

'My reward is in heaven, John. And in seeing decent young men like you rise to positions of power.'

'Thank you. I don't know what else to say.'

Neither of us said anything for a while, then Mary broke the silence.

'Something's bothering you, John. What would you like to ask me?'

'You're right, Mary. Can I ask you a question?'

'Of course. I don't promise to give you an answer.'

'I understand that.'

She looked at me, unblinkingly. 'Go on, then.'

I took a deep breath. 'The bank actually knew exactly how much money went into Scotty Livingston's rucksack.'

Mary said nothing.

'The thing is, Mary, that the rucksack had £480 less in it than there should have been.'

Still she said nothing. I wondered if I'd gone too far.

Eventually Mary spoke. 'What do you want to ask me, John?' she said, coolly. Then she relaxed a little. 'It's all right, John. Whatever you want to ask me, I forgive you in advance.'

I took yet another deep breath.

'Personally, I've no problem that £480 is missing. Even the bank is happy to write it off given that no one was hurt. And I know you have… expenses to meet.'

A quiet smile returned to Mary's face. I knew the crisis was past.

'You still haven't asked your question yet, John.'

'That dress… there's nowhere you could possibly hide any money. Is there? It would show.'

Mary smiled again. I could tell she was hatching something. Eventually she said, 'Would you like see if it's possible?'

Alarmed, I reassured Mary that I had no wish to see any of her innermost secrets.

'I know that, John. You're too much of a gentleman. But you have a professional curiosity, don't you?'

I gulped. 'Yes.' I'd no idea where I was going. 'Please, Mary, I'm only asking the question.'

'Do you have a ten pound note?'

Slightly taken aback, I reached for my wallet and handed one over. Mary took it, reached discreetly down the neckline of her dress – today's was a deep green shade – and placed it in her cleavage. Like every other part of her, the form of the ten pound note could clearly be seen. She'd made her point.

Mary recovered my ten pound note as gracefully as she'd hidden it.

'If you care to look away for a moment, John, I could try and hide it somewhere at my back.' She bent down as if to roll up her dress, much as she'd done with Scotty Livingston.

'That absolutely won't be necessary, Mary. You've already answered my question. I'm sorry I felt the need to ask.'

'I told you, John, you were free to ask me anything. Are you any further forward with your enquiries?' Just to confuse me still further, at the same time she handed back the ten pound note. It was already infused with a mixture of scents, one of which was of course Chanel No 5.

'No,' I said, 'I've still no idea how that money left the bank. But as I said, I don't mind, at least I don't mind if it ended up in your hands. You deserve it. And a great deal more, to be honest.' That brought yet another mysterious smile from Mary.

We exchanged a few more details about other matters, then I said I'd have to leave. As she led me to the door, I had one last chance to notice that there was no way she could have secreted any money on her person that day. And as that day, she was barefoot: once again, she'd left her shoes by the front door. She asked visitors like me to do the same, which gave me a moment longer as I knelt beside her to tie my laces.

It was then it occurred to me: the shoes, of course.

As I stood up, Mary caught the grin on my face.

'You seem happy, John. Have you solved your problem?'

'I think so, Mary. Thank you for asking.'

'Not at all, John. I'm delighted to have been able to be of service.'

'Oh, you're *definitely* of service, Mary. Definitely.'

THE JEWEL THIEF

Chauffeuring Sister Mary Maxwell-Hume, of the Sisters of Mary of the Sacred Cross, was not without its hazards. She wasn't difficult to spot, sitting as she often did in the passenger seat of my Smart patrol car, and I was afraid that my superiors would upbraid me for giving a member of the public such easy access to police transport.

Actually, only one 'superior' really cared. Amongst most of my colleagues, the word was already out that Mary Maxwell-Hume had helped me out several times. Sometimes she solved petty crimes, sometimes she averted a crisis; most of all, though, she brought me a sense of perspective and made me better at my job. I'd also learned that Sister Mary might have been a little bit of a rogue herself, but she was courageous. I suppose any nun who lives by a mantra that requires that she and her fellow Sisters 'wear only as much clothing as is necessary to provide due modesty' has to have a little brass neck.

The one senior officer who strongly disapproved of Mary was Inspector Maximilian Plews. Plews would have loved it if one of his superiors would have called him 'Max', but they despised him as much as he despised those under his command. Naturally, no one junior to Plews was allowed to address him other than as 'Inspector', or 'Sir'.

Plews and Mary had history; his brother Theodore was director at Lambert's Auction House on the outskirts of Edinburgh and had more than once made complaints about her. Usually, though, I was sent to deal with the problem. Theodore ('Teddy') Plews was an odious little man who wore dapper suits, a permanent sneer and a Hitler moustache in no particular order. His older brother Maximilian was slightly taller, had no moustache, and was a little bulkier; otherwise they were like two peas in a pod. Naturally, I only ever saw Inspector Plews in uniform, but he was rumoured to wear three-piece suits on his days off.

Sister Mary Maxwell-Hume of the Sisters of the Sacred Cross was actually banned from Lambert's. Accordingly, she took great delight in disguising herself to gain entry – which sometimes also meant that she had to bend the Order's rule that the Sisters should 'wear only as much clothing as is necessary to preserve modesty.' It was a little game that she liked to play, which she almost always concluded by revealing herself through olfactory routes: she allowed Theodore Plews to be aware of her Chanel No.5 perfume. His face, rewardingly, would immediately change through a series of shades of red towards a deep puce, but he was rarely able to speak, such was his rage. I remember once suggesting to Mary that her behaviour might be less than Christian, but she replied by reeling off a raft of examples from the Bible where Jesus and others were rightfully furious with unrepentant sinners. And it was hard to feel the slightest sympathy for either Theodore Plews or his brother.

When Mary discovered that brother Maximilian was a few steps up the food chain from me, she became enormously interested.

'How wonderful! If only we could make both of their lives miserable at the same time.'

I suggested that she might be indulging in a little wishful thinking.

'The Lord will provide! The Lord will provide!' Knowing Mary, I had a feeling that 'the Lord' might need – and receive – a little assistance.

Inspector Plews, of Edinburgh 'B' Division, sat in his office and raged. Like most offices in the recently renovated building, his had a glass wall; it meant that he could see out, to be sure, but the strong internal light made him look like a goldfish in a bowl. Everyone simply left him to it.

Plews had just been summoned to the office of his own superior, Superintendent Jack O'Malley. O'Malley was from somewhere in the west of Scotland – not Glasgow, perhaps the Motherwell area – and was a 'has-wenter'. If you're not familiar with lowland Scottish dialect, many people from those parts simply speak differently from their Edinburgh, Aberdeen, Border or Highland cousins. Many linguistics experts have suggested that the west-coast dialect is actually derived heavily from Old Norman French: for instance, the word 'you' is almost always spoken in the plural, 'youz'. For men like the Plews brothers who had attended a fee-paying school and received lessons in Latin and Greek, people like Jack O'Malley were simply ignorant, pointing out that in Latin the word simply means 'they know nothing'.

O'Malley compounded his crimes by being a die-hard supporter of Celtic Football Club. He timed his leave days to coincide with the glamour midweek European ties, not minding too much if he had to work a weekend to compensate. Plews assumed that he was a Roman Catholic; in fact, O'Malley 'couldnaez gi' a', showing a little restraint by never completing the phrase with the standard expletive. Technically O'Malley was married, with two children at university, but his wife had long since left him for an oil worker and O'Malley's view of marriage, the sanctity of its vows, and of churches in general, was a little jaundiced. He and Sister Mary had never met, but I'd long wondered what would happen if they ever did.

O'Malley was, however, a top class police officer.

Plews' visit to O'Malley's office had not gone well. O'Malley was angry that Plews seemed to be making no progress whatsoever in bringing a spate of jewellery thefts to an end.

'Jeez, Plews, yes ken whae done it. We a' ken it's Compass.' James Compass was a suave operator but a known villain. 'Pull him in.'

Plews stiffened. He'd not been invited to sit down, so a 'stiff' Theodore Plews reached all the way to the giddy heights of five feet six inches. Perhaps half an inch less, given that he was bald these days. O'Malley was seated at his desk, and Plews stared directly in front of him, so that he was addressing the wall above O'Malley's head.

'I don't have the evidence, sir.'

O'Malley stood up and stared at him unblinkingly. Suddenly he slammed his hand down hard on his desk and yelled, 'WELL GO OUT AND FIND SOME, YA BALD MORON! This has went on far tae long. Ah dinnae care how youz dae it, but dinnae cam back here wi'out his head on a plate! Set him up if ye have tae.'

'Yez're – I mean, you're not serious?' Plews said. 'Plant stuff on him?'

'No' literally, ya daft lummox.' Plews had no idea what a 'lummox' was, but it didn't sound like a compliment. 'Compass has tae steal the jewellery frae somewhere, and he has tae sell it oan somewhere else. Sooner or later it has tae appear in a shop, or in an auction somewhere. Hae a team in place at the next jewellery auction. He's aye at thae things. Dae yez unnerstand?'

'Yes, sir,' Plews replied, although in truth he would have liked a translator present.

*

Everyone avoided Inspector Maximilian Plews when he was in a bad mood; in fact they tried to avoid him no matter what mood he was in. So when the Inspector called out, 'PC Knox! In here, straight away', I wasn't looking forward to what lay in store.

'Yes, sir?'

'Knox, I don't suppose a man of your limited horizons will have heard of the auction house, Lambert's. It used to be in the city centre but has moved out to a modern building on the outskirts of the city. It sells quality art products, music, jewellery, antique furniture, old clocks and so on. Not the sort of stuff I'd expect you to understand.'

I decided to let him have his little dig. 'No, sir.'

'The Superintendent wants us to catch this Compass fellow once and for all. I'd like you to go to a jewellery sale there next Tuesday. As it happens, my brother is the Director there, so he'll show you what's what. We'd like to lift Compass red-handed.'

'Do I go in uniform, sir?'

'Of course you wear uniform, Constable. What were you planning on wearing, your pyjamas?' Plews thought he was being funny, so I thought it safest to chuckle. 'I just wondered if I shouldn't be more incognito.'

'Uniform.'

'As you say, sir. Whatever you and the Superintendent would like.'

A flicker of doubt passed across Plews' face. He rose from his seat, went into O'Malley's office, and clearly asked about my uniform. Even through the thick glass walls and doors, I could hear O'Malley's answer, the more so because O'Malley was still yelling at Plews as the door opened.

'Ye stupid, clueless – '

Plews quickly closed the door behind him to block out

the noise. 'Plain clothes, Knox. The Superintendent changed his mind.'

'As you wish, sir,' I said.

'I'm counting on you to catch this man red-handed, Knox,' Plews said.

'On my own, sir?'

'You're an experienced officer, Knox. Do you need help?' I was about to suggest that another officer would be useful when he looked down at the paperwork on his desk and said 'I hope not.'

The conversation had ended. Plews didn't look up, started writing again, and didn't grace me with any further communication.

I picked up the bulky file on James Compass. A smooth operator, he was known for his aversion to getting caught. His technique was actually fairly simple: he didn't steal particularly valuable items, simply a great many of modest worth. When sold on, the wedding and engagement rings, bracelets, brooches and coins and medals were not important enough to attract attention from second-hand dealers. If a dealer did realise that an item was stolen, it was simply safer to say nothing to the police at all. Experience had shown that the first police move would be to try and charge any dealer with fencing the goods. That was actually Plews' approach – he believed in trying to terrify potential witnesses into saying whatever he wanted them to say.

The jewellery itself might be stolen from from the owners' persons, their homes, or from shops, even from market stalls and exhibitions, but there was one place Compass simply couldn't resist: auction salerooms. As elsewhere, he targeted attractive but modest pieces, not those of the highest value.

That evening, I was having my weekly piano lesson with Mary Maxwell-Hume, and I mentioned the new task I'd been landed with.

'So your Inspector Plews, John – he wants you to catch this jewel thief Mr Compass at his brother's auction house? All on your own?'

'That about sums it up. Then he takes the glory for thinking up the idea in the first place.'

She instructed me to play a scale of F harmonic minor on the piano, four octaves, both hands simultaneously. It wasn't very good, I admit.

'Oh my, John, that will never do. Would you like some help?'

Thinking we were discussing the F minor scale, I wondered if she was planning some sort of duet version. But I was on the wrong track.

'Would you like me to come with you and offer a little assistance with your jewellery thief?'

I was a little thrown. 'By coming to Lambert's Auction House, you mean? I thought you were banned.' Sister Mary and Theodore Plews, Lambert's Edinburgh director, did not enjoy good relations.

'Being banned hasn't stopped me in the past, has it?'

I grinned. 'No, it hasn't, Mary. It takes more than a ban to stop you.'

Mary summoned me for an 'extra piano lesson' on Sunday afternoon, two days before the jewellery sale at Lambert's. I was asked to bring a photograph and a description of Compass, and to make sure that I could provide her with a few details of his methods, his preferred types of jewellery. I explained that Compass would often bid for high-value lots, but wouldn't actually try to put in a winning bid. Instead, he was interested in little boxes of uninteresting wedding rings, budget engagement rings and silver bracelets. They would be displayed during their auction, but then returned to the box until the auction came to an end. Compass' technique wasn't quite clear, but when the successful bidder went forward to pay and collect the items, the box proved to be empty.

'How do you know it's this man Compass?' Mary asked me after a particularly excruciating rendition of Chopin's *Prelude No. 15 in D flat.*

'We don't, really. We've never seen him. It's just that the particular method only ever happens when Compass is present.'

She signalled that I should torture the Chopin again. 'And how many thefts have taken place?'

'Thirty-four.'

'What? That's awful,' she cried, and burst out laughing. Briefly, I stopped playing for a moment, which only allowed Mary to remind me that my playing was both awful and laughable, too, but at was at least legal. Just and no more.

'That's thirty-four magic boxes that make jewellery disappear?'

'That's one possible solution, I suppose,' I admitted. 'But it's not a line the police are actively following up, I have to admit.'

'How many of the thirty-four have taken place at Lambert's?'

'All thirty-four of them,' I admitted. 'He seems to have it in for your Mr Plews.'

'Oh well then, Compass can't be all bad. Play!'

Prelude No. 15 was even worse second time around, but Mary's mind seemed to be on other things, and her thoughts were far from piano music when I finished.

'This Compass fellow,' Mary said. 'You say he appears to work alone?'

'So it seems. Perhaps he doesn't. No one has clue how he does it. Nor do we know how he gets the stolen goods out of Lambert's.'

'He must have some help, I think,' Mary said. She came across, sat beside me on the piano stool but with her back to the piano, and added. 'Perhaps he has inside help?'

'I did ask the Inspector that, and he simply erupted.' I filled Mary in with the details of the ear-bashing I'd received. Was I suggesting that his brother Theodore was a poor judge of staff integrity, he'd demanded to know?

'I suspect the Plews brothers are rather unfamiliar with the concept of integrity,' she suggested. I remained silent, thinking of some of Sister Mary's own past exploits. 'So it's just you and I, John, is it?'

I gulped. 'Not quite.'

'Well?'

'There's this thing going on between the Inspector and Superintendent O'Malley. O'Malley's threatened to have Plews transferred to the Children's Road Safety Unit if this isn't solved quickly. On Tuesday, in fact.'

'Oh that sounds awful,' said Mary. 'Those poor children…'

'And although O'Malley and Inspector Plews are going to be in the sale room as potential buyers, it's to be my job to catch Compass red-handed. You know, I've never seen the Inspector out of uniform.'

'Oh how horrible for you, John! But we must save those children from Inspector Plews!'

'I'm counting on you, Mary.'

Mary sat for a while beside me on the piano stool, thinking. 'I need an all-over massage, John. Will you give me one?'

I stared at her, transfixed. Perhaps I'd had an overdose of Chanel No.5.

'Massage me on the piano, John. Chopin, *Prelude No. 15 in D flat*. From the top, please.'

It did sound a little better this time.

Two days later, the monthly Lambert's jewellery auction began. Some of the staff were surprised to see Theodore Plews there at all, given that no individual item of major value was up for sale. They were even more surprised to see their Director standing beside someone who, apart from an enhanced girth and the absence of a moustache, appeared to be his exact double. To Maximilian's right stood Jack O'Malley. The latter had already fallen foul of an elderly lady with a large handbag who had asked him to put out his cigarette – to which O'Malley had responded by stubbing it out on the saleroom floor.

I'd positioned myself near the middle of the room, well away from my senior colleagues. I wanted to concentrate on my job, I didn't want to engage in any more conversation with either of them than I could help, but most of all because the pair of them were an embarrassment to the police force. On the positive side, being an embarrassment meant that they would never fool anyone for serving policemen.

There was no sign of Mary Maxwell-Hume, however. I looked all around for her, but after all she was simply a member of the public: even if I were disappointed, I had no right to expect her to be there. I'd have to solve this on my own, and with an audience of two of my superiors watching.

James Compass was standing right at the front. Clearly, then, he had some method of snatching the jewels while no one was looking, as he could almost reach out and touch them. For the next hour, I watched intently as he drifted around close to, but not quite close enough to, the various lots.

Around 11.30, a series of lots came up which, from the catalogue, I'd suspected might be of interest to Compass. There were five collections of 'assorted jewellery', loosely arranged into 'items with small diamonds', 'gold rings' 'platinum items', 'assorted bracelets, rings and earrings' and 'assorted small items'. A gentleman on the floor beside me explained that none of the individual pieces was of great worth on its own, but small-scale dealers traded them online or through backstreet dealers. However, the total value of the jewellery could add up to quite a lot in the hands of an experienced trader prepared to hold out for good prices.

Compass bid for the gold rings and the platinum items, but nothing else. Predictably, his bids were low, however, and he dropped out early, allowing others to win. The gold and platinum lots sold for several thousands, the others for a lot less.

And then the sale was over. Compass had bid for a couple of items, bought nothing at all, and I was left wondering what I was supposed to be watching. At the end, successful buyers – of whom Compass was not one, of course – were asked to come forward to settle up. I looked round at the Superintendent and the Inspector and shrugged my shoulders. They shrugged their shoulders back at me. Director Theodore Plews, on the other hand, seemed to assume that his man was about to be captured.

I was about to give up when I heard a voice behind me.

'Ah. Watch, John. Watch.' It was the elderly lady.

She whispered again that I should pay careful attention to what was going on at the front. The auction clerk – an attractive brunette who appeared to be in her early forties – was taking the money and handing over the lots to the successful bidders was asking each one to sign a ledger to say that they'd received their goods. As each person signed, there was a brief moment as she leant over to point out the correct place in the ledger.

Then I saw it. As one of the successful bidders was signing, an elderly man who was buying an antique engagement ring, the auction clerk slipped the entire contents of one of the 'assorted jewellery' boxes into a side pocket of his sports jacket, closed the box, and returned to her work. She completed the entire movement without a sound in less than three seconds, and the elderly gentleman knew nothing of it at all. Nor, it transpired, did either of the Plews brothers or O'Malley.

I was about to intervene when the elderly lady beside me pulled me back. I couldn't see her, but her Chanel No.5 told me all I needed to know.

'I need to do something, John,' she said. 'As that elderly man passes, ask to see the ring he's just bought. I'm sure he'll be glad to show you.'

Mary slipped forwards unnoticed, and as she did so accidentally walked directly into the elderly new owner of the engagement ring. Each apologised profusely to the other, then each carried on their way. Eventually, his route to the exit took him past me.

'Even from this distance, that looks a lovely ring,' I said. 'Is it for someone special?'

The elderly gentleman smiled at me. 'Thank you, yes it is. My wife and I will celebrate our golden wedding anniversary shortly. We never actually got engaged, so I thought it would be nice finally to do so to mark the occasion.' He opened the little box to let me see it more closely. 'I know she'd prefer something that's been rescued, though, so I'm going to get it re-engraved.'

'That's a lovely story,' I said. 'Congratulations. I hope you both have a wonderful day.' In the background, I could see Compass watching us both closely. I'd lost sight of Mary for the moment.

Suddenly there was a yell from the front.

'Mr Plews! Mr Plews! It's happened again! Something's been stolen! It's a box of silver bracelets and earrings this time.' It was the auction clerk, frantically waving for attention. Compass tried to escape, but when he got there, his route was blocked by the elderly lady, who – rather clumsily – appeared to be adjusting her footwear.

Compass simply couldn't get past, so he tried to push through, causing the elderly lady to yell for help. That was obviously my cue, and I grabbed his arm.

'Excuse me, sir, you seem to be in a hurry to leave.'

Compass growled at me. 'And who do you think you are?'

I produced my warrant card. 'Hasn't the auction clerk just shouted that something has been stolen?'

Compass sneered at me. 'I hope you're not suggesting that I'm the thief. Perhaps you'd like to search me?'

By now he'd attracted everyone's attention, and Superintendent O'Malley and Inspector Plews had joined us.

'I hope you've got this right, Knox,' Plews said. 'We don't want someone suing us for wrongful arrest.'

'No, you don't,' Compass agreed. I was worried, but I noticed that the auction clerk looked even more concerned.

'May I search your pockets, sir?' I asked, as politely as I could.

'Go ahead,' Compass said.

His left jacket pocket contained nothing, but the right hand one was full of bracelets, some rings, and several pairs of earrings. Compass looked crestfallen.

'But…'

Inspector Plews produced his warrant card and announced

grandly that he was arresting Compass on suspicion of theft. I had to prompt him on the exact wording of the rights warning, but he was determined to claim it as his 'collar'. I mentioned quietly to the Superintendent that the auction clerk should be detained, too. Mary, meanwhile, was calming the elderly man down; they looked like any other couple in their late seventies.

I asked Theodore Plews to accompany me to the front to speak to the auction clerk: he was, after all her boss. Plews was still fuming that one of his employees was under suspicion. But the woman didn't resist. I explained that I'd seen everything, and she just crumbled. She told me her name, Louisa Lomax, and her age, 42.

'Look,' she added, 'you're going to find out anyway. Lomax is my maiden name. I use it at work.'

I looked at her. 'Go on.'

'My married name is Compass. James and I are married. I do love him, you know. We'll cooperate, I'll make sure James will, too. I don't look forward to jail.'

Plews looked at her, disgusted. 'How could you, Miss Lomax – or what ever you are? Have you no shame?'

I turned towards Plews. 'Don't you do background checks on your staff, sir?'

Plews didn't reply; he simply turned a deeper shade of red.

A squad car with two uniformed officers was summoned to remove the villainous couple. Standing outside with yet another cigarette in his mouth, O'Malley patted me on the back.

'Well done, lad. You saved your boss from the Children's Road Safety Unit. You'll be coming back the station to fill out your report straight away?'

'If you don't mind, sir,' I said, 'I should give this elderly lady a lift home. She's had a bit of a shock.'

'That's a good idea, son. Good public relations.' He leaned across towards the lady in question. 'I hope you don't mind me smoking outside, madam, do you?'

'It's not a nice habit, but it's not against the law,' Mary said sharply. Then she softened her tone a little and asked, 'By the way, that man across there in the too-tight suit. Is he a policeman, too?'

'Yes, madam, that's Inspector Plews.'

'Why does he have a silver necklace hanging out of his jacket pocket?'

O'Malley looked closely. 'That, Madam, is a very good question. One I'd like to know the answer to.'

'I'll leave you find out, then,' Mary said.

It was a relief to get back to my Smart patrol car. For once, ferrying Mary home didn't seem a burden at all, and she'd certainly earned the lift. First, though, she needed to remove some clothing, it seemed. I offered to look away, but she insisted it wasn't required.

'Thank you for all your help, Mary,' I said, as she removed a brown skirt, jumper and jacket to reveal something altogether more familiar underneath: a red crepe close-fitting dress. As the skirt came off, she let the dress underneath drop – she'd rolled the red dress up to waist level, using it to give herself exaggerated hips. Now all the surplus clothing was being stuffed into her large holdall.

'Not at all,' Mary said, smoothing down the crepe dress. As she did so, it almost felt reassuring to see her return to her normal form. And as usual, her quiet smile indicated that she knew what was in my mind.

'I've gained a few brownie points, thanks to you,' I said. 'The Inspector thinks I solved the crime all on my own.'

'Yet he claimed the arrest for himself?'

'That's how it works, sometimes, Mary. Officers like me are at the bottom of the food chain, I'm afraid.'

By now we were in the patrol car, and Mary reached under the passenger seat back for her supply of Chanel No.5 before dabbing a little more on her wrists, and behind her ears. I was aware that something about her was different, though, and then I realised what it was.

'Mary…'

'Yes, John?' She had returned to avoiding my gaze and looking out of the passenger-side window of the patrol car.

'Those earrings? Were you wearing them when you arrived at the auction house?'

'I've only recently acquired them,' she said, not quite answering my question. 'Do you like them?'

I had to admit that they looked lovely earrings: silver drop, a couple of tiny diamonds, and a ruby in each. They might well have been worth several hundred pounds, but on Mary, with her red dress, they looked to be worth a fortune. Indeed, one way or another, Sister Mary Maxwell-Hume appeared to be gaining more value every time we met.

THE COCKTAIL PARTY

Rather against the better judgement of its Director Theodore Plews, Lambert's Auction House held the occasional cocktail party for its more honoured guests. Company policy was never to sell anything at a cocktail party, although of course some of the more interesting lots for forthcoming sales would invariably be on display. Lambert's prided itself on being a modern, 21st century setup, with video monitors, electronic displays of the current bid and any number of facilities – even a nappy-changing room.

Even from my limited experience of Theodore Plews, I wasn't surprised to learn that he regarded this 'modernisation' process as entirely needless. More than once I'd heard Plews describe himself as a 'traditionalist', but like most self-styled traditionalists, that only meant that he felt threatened by change of any sort. The biggest change in recent years had been the relocation of Lambert's Edinburgh from its traditional – there's that word again – home in the city centre to this new purpose-built building on the outskirts. Driven primarily by Bethany Helm, Lambert's extremely talented Head of Development UK, the move had been a major success. The new Lambert's sat less than ten minutes' drive from the airport, and just a short walk from a choice of three large brand-new hotels.

It was Bethany Helm's idea to hold the cocktail parties. Concerned that a building on the outskirts might put off local buyers, she laid on a series of free events, complete with minibus transport home to various parts of the city afterwards. For the locals, the combination of high-class canapés, free drink, not having to worry about driving home, and the chance to rub shoulders with the great and good of Edinburgh society was irresistible. And, costly to put on as these cocktail evenings might at first seem, Bethany argued that one or two extra decent sales commissions would more than justify the costs. And she was proving to be right.

Although based in Edinburgh, Bethany Helm wasn't Scottish, she was from somewhere in Greater London. On appointment, her first task had been to oversee the new Lambert's Edinburgh construction, and headquarters had decided that some surplus custom-built office space in the new building would be far more suitable for the Head of Development UK than anything in London.

I'd met Bethany Helm a couple of times and I knew straight away that she and Theodore Plews wouldn't get on. Neither she nor Plews was directly responsible to the other, something that pleased the Director not one bit. For her part, Bethany, a young woman not yet thirty years old, wasn't afraid to speak her mind; nor was she averse to using her undoubted ability to charm people – men, especially – to get her way. To start with, she even tried to chat Plews up, but with predictable results: Plews might be a pompous, aggressive little Hitler of a man, but he was no adulterer. Bethany was therefore forced to turn to Plan B, which was to expose the man as an ignorant boor. There she was on safer ground.

Bethany, it seemed, was taking every opportunity to relay stories of Plews' incompetence or unpleasantness to London HQ. She was ably supported by most of Lambert's staff, almost all of whom had experienced Plews at his worst. Earlier in the week of the cocktail party, for instance, he had refused permission to his furniture expert Andy Lismore to be with his seriously ill child in hospital; it was 'the mother's job', according to Plews. Bethany herself had more than once been asked to 'smarten up' in the saleroom, by which Plews meant 'wear a decent black skirt and a white blouse'. No trousers. He'd even once suggested that customers might prefer it if she lost some weight. Naturally, she ignored him, which enraged Plews still further. Instead, Bethany made no secret of the fact that she felt she would like Plews' job, that she could take command of an auction house herself. Many of her Lambert's Edinburgh colleagues longed for that very thing to happen.

Uptake of invitations to the October cocktail party was even larger than usual. Bethany had sent out cards to all the usual mailing list, but because the party was scheduled for 6.00 p.m. on a Friday evening, she'd added in a few senior Scottish politicians for good measure. Three Scottish Cabinet ministers were present; four MPs had shown up, too, each drawn by the prospect of free drink and private taxis at Lambert's expense. Their presence had in turn drawn many of the business community. All these stellar attendees naturally attracted ordinary members of the public in like moths to a light. The public would all be going home together in buses, though: no taxis for the hoi-polloi.

In addition, three officers from Police Scotland had been specially invited: Superintendent Jack O'Malley; Inspector Maximilian Plews (co-incidentally, the brother of the auction house Director); and me. Plews and O'Malley had recently gained fame for capturing the infamous jewel thief James Compass and his accomplice, as well as solving the mystery of how their crimes were being committed. The capture had actually taken place in this very auction room just two months previously, and this was Lambert's way of saying thank you to O'Malley and Plews. Politicians, business leaders, the ordinary public – they were all there to celebrate these two famous policemen. I myself had played a small but seemingly forgotten role in the capture of James Compass, but this evening, the public assumed that I was there simply to act as the senior policemen's assistant. For my two superiors, that was probably what they thought as well.

The evening began with Theodore Plews welcoming everyone present and introducing 'the honoured guests' one by one, until eventually he reached O'Malley and Plews. Plews introduced his brother as 'the real Sherlock Holmes of the Compass case', while O'Malley was introduced as his 'superior officer'. The warm round of applause that Inspector Maximilian Plews received might well have been the first applause he'd received in fifteen years. I'd never heard anyone praise him, at any rate.

O'Malley was clearly miffed that Theodore was talking up the role of his brother Maximilian. Whoever had actually done the hard work on the ground, O'Malley believed it took even more talent to delegate it. But Inspector Maximilian Plews and he had previously agreed to share the credit for the arrest and now Plews was taking it all.

Pushing his inspector aside, the superintendent stepped forward to say a few quick words. Many of those present knew that O'Malley's words would be in something only distantly related to the English language.

'Speakin' on behalfs o' a' us yins at Police Scotland' – he said 'Police Scoatland' slowly and clearly – 'I'd like tae say thanks tae a' fur the kind wurds. Of course it's a team effort, and as team... captain... I feel proud tae hae led the investigation tae such a successful conclusion.' He waved at his inspector. 'I'm sure Inspector Plews here wid fully agree wi' me that he wiz just a small coag in a very big wheel.'

It was clear that the inspector agreed no such thing, but

he could hardly argue with his superior officer in public. Instead, the colour of his ample face and neck simply turned a slightly deeper shade of purple.

Then it was Bethany's turn. She bounced enthusiastically onto the small raised dais, and gave a brief rundown of the various services that Lambert's offered, as well as some of the forthcoming auctions: paintings, clocks, coins and medals, and silverware. She made a little joke about the attempted theft during the recent jewellery auction. The audience found it funny, but not Theodore Plews, who would rather the event had never happened at all in his personal auction room. Then she simply invited everyone to enjoy themselves.

Bethany Helm's work was only just beginning, however. Her role was to circulate, to work the room, ensuring that each of the star guests felt suitably attended to. I studied her activity from a distance.

'It's amazing, isn't it?'

An elderly hunch-backed lady stood beside me. Her hair might have been tinted jet black. She might once have been quite tall, but doubled over, her height had reduced by a quarter at least. She wore a long open red coat, her hands thrust in its pockets. None of which was normal for Mary Maxwell-Hume. I was used to seeing her dressed in one of her famous elegant close-fitting dresses that showed none of her body and everything at the same time. Only her Chanel No.5 reassured me that I was in the company of Sister Mary of the Sisters of the Sacred Cross.

'What's amazing, Mary?' I asked. I didn't need to ask why she was in disguise: Theodore Plews had banned Mary Maxwell-Hume from Lambert's Auction House. They didn't quite see eye-to-eye.

'That young woman – Bethany, is that her name? – is working the room with extraordinary efficiency. If you watch her, each politician is being given two minutes, each of the business leaders and other worthies 90 seconds each, and everyone else is getting nods, 'hellos', the odd hug or kiss. She has every single person in the room mapped out.'

'Even ourselves?'

'Oh no,' Mary said. 'She won't come to us.'

'Because?'

'Because we're going to move round the room ourselves to annoy her,' Mary said, much to my amusement. 'Anyway, John, you'll be offered more canapés and wine if you keep moving than if you stand still.'

For all that Mary seemed to be having a little fun, I was interested to see how much attention she was paying to Bethany's movements. All the tables and little ledges in the room were being fully utilised as guests set down glasses of champagne, paper plates or empty cocktail sticks. Bethany herself frequently picked her glass up and laid it down, mainly because she preferred to use both hands to greet people: for a hug or a double kiss on the cheek, she naturally needed both; but even her handshake involved a little touch on the sleeve with the left hand. Bethany Helm was touchy-feely. And her guests loved it.

Theodore Plews was less impressed. He found such behaviour distasteful, even unprofessional; but then his contempt for Bethany was as obvious as hers was for him. Jack O'Malley didn't find a hug from Bethany Helm distasteful at all, indeed he found plenty of Bethany to keep a hold of, and for rather longer than was appropriate. His colleague Inspector Maximilian Plews settled for a handshake, in part because he was standing right beside Theodore at that point. Bethany chatted for her mandatory 120 seconds to each, then moved on, champagne glass in hand. Not that she had had much time to drink much of it.

A few minutes later, Bethany stopped.

'Ah,' said Mary quietly to me. 'She's counting. She's not got everyone.'

'Us?'

'Us, John. What fun.'

We watched as Bethany looked about the room, wondering who it was that she had still to glad-hand. Just then, she was accosted by one of the other guests, she took a decent drink from her champagne and turned to speak to them with a broad smile.

The broad smile didn't last long. Instead, her face froze, and she started gasping in agony.

'No...!' she said, doubling over.

At first the room was so busy that her misfortune went unnoticed by almost anyone except for the bewildered couple who had waved her over. But one other person had been watching.

Suddenly, the elderly hunch-backed lady who had been standing beside me vanished and transformed into a tallish, elegant silver-haired woman wearing a deep red dress which revealed everything and nothing all at once. She'd kicked off her sandals and in seconds was beside Bethany. She took a sniff of the champagne.

'She's drunk bleach, John!' Mary shouted across to me. 'Get some water, milk, anything! Quick!'

The waiters were carrying some soft drinks, including jugs of water. I grabbed whatever I could, then instructed them to go and find as much more as possible immediately.

Bethany was kneeling on the floor, trying to cough up what she'd drunk. All she could say was 'Plews, Plews...'

Meanwhile, O'Malley and the inspector did what I was most used to seeing them do: nothing. Theodore Plews, on the other hand, was apoplectic with rage at this most serious turn of events.

'WHAT'S THAT WOMAN DOING HERE?' he asked.

One of the staff tried to explain that it was actually Bethany Helm who had been poisoned.

'I DON'T CARE ABOUT HER! HOW DID THAT WOMAN' – he pointed at Mary – 'GET IN HERE? GET HER OUT NOW!!' he screamed.

Bethany, meantime, was drinking water and still repeating 'Plews, Plews…' An ambulance had been called. Finally, the two senior policemen made their way towards the action.

'Someone appears to have added bleach to Ms Helm's champagne,' I explained.

'You think they tried to kill her, son?' O'Malley asked.

'Why else would anyone add bleach to a glass of champagne, sir?'

'Who'd want to harm Ms Helm?' O'Malley asked.

By now, Theodore had joined his brother, O'Malley, Mary and me as we tried to minister to Bethany. Someone had already called an ambulance. Theodore Plews simply seemed to regard Bethany as a stain on the floor; everyone could see his look of disgust. Now, instead of worrying about Bethany, the gathered staff and guests were staring at the one person present who might definitely want to harm her: Theodore Lancelot Plews.

On the floor, Bethany was still coughing, 'Plews, Plews, Plews…'

Superintendent Jack O'Malley saw his chance to make a high-profile public arrest. It would look good in a press release, he knew: 'The Police Superintendent Who's Still In Touch With The Bobby On The Beat.' Even Inspector Maximilian Plews recognised that things looked bad for his brother.

O'Malley turned to face Theodore Plews.

'Theodore Plews, someone has tried to kill Ms Helm here. You had the motive and the opportunity to commit the crime and I'm arresting you in connection with it. You're not obliged to say anything…,' then suddenly realised that he didn't know the rest of the caution by heart; he had to ask me to finish it for him. Normally, someone like O'Malley would have delegated me to handcuff Plews and lead him away, but the superintendent wanted the public to see him being 'a real copper'. He knew that photos and video of the arrest would be on social media in seconds.

As O'Malley stepped forward to grab the stunned-looking auction house director, Mary stood up and whispered 'the lipstick' in my ear. It was my turn to be a little bemused now, not least because, close up, Sister Mary Maxwell-Hume can be an extremely distracting influence on any man. Thankfully I was still too busy to take in her dress, but of course there was still the Chanel No.5.

'The lipstick, John, the lipstick,' she repeated. 'Pay attention.'

I still didn't get it.

'There's lipstick on two glasses, John.' She pointed to another glass where Theodore Plews had been standing. 'It's the same lipstick – I can tell from here.'

It took me a moment to realise what she was saying.

'Did you see it happen?' I asked Mary.

'Of course. But I didn't know it was bleach, of course. Just a little plastic phial of a clear liquid. I needed to smell the bleach in the champagne.' She whispered a few more details in my ear, then she added aloud, 'Quick. You haven't much time.'

O'Malley and Theodore Plews were almost at the exit door, with Maximilian in their wake.

'Sir!' I yelled. 'Sir! Wait a minute, please!'

Clearly irritated, O'Malley looked round.

'What is it, son? Dinnae you be wastin' ma time right now o' a' times.'

'I wonder if there's another possibility, sir?'

O'Malley looked furious. Inspector Maximilian Plews looked torn: torn between not wishing to be associated with a murderous brother; or his contempt for police low-life such as me. To make things worse, this entire scene was being played out in front of a large and utterly rapt audience.

'Superintendent,' Mary called out. 'I'm very impressed with the constable's powers of observation. Perhaps you should hear him out.'

O'Malley looked at his inspector, then back towards me.

'Go on, then. Let's all hear it, Sherlock Holmes.'

'It's the lipstick, sir.'

'The lipstick?'

'There's lipstick on two glasses. Ms Helm's original one, and the glass belonging to Mr Plews, Lambert's Director.'

'So?'

'It's Ms Helm's lipstick on both glasses. The two drinks got mixed up when she put her one down to add the bleach to Mr Plews' glass.'

'Yez are saying Ms Helm added the bleach tae her ain drink?' O'Malley asked.

'Not deliberately, she got mixed up. She was trying to poison Mr Theodore Plews.' Everyone looked down at Bethany Helm, who was sitting up on the floor. The water seemed to be helping her, but now tears were pouring down her cheeks.

I tried to make things a little clearer. 'I think forensics will show that the only person in the room who's had any contact with bleach is Ms Helm herself.'

'Help me, please,' Bethany gasped. 'I'm sorry. Please help

me.'

'There's an ambulance on the way, Ms Helm,' O'Malley said. 'But you tried to kill someone – are we supposed to feel sorry for you?'

'I wasn't trying to kill Mr Plews, just to put him out of action for a while.'

'It comes to the same thing in a court of law. Read the woman her rights, Knox.' I did so, then he nodded to Theodore Plews. 'Looks like the constable's done yez a favour, Mr Plews – yez are in the clear. But keep oot o' ma road for the rest of night, please.' The Director was too relieved to argue. He turned around and left straight away.

Then O'Malley turned to Maximilian Plews and said. 'I think we should try and get this woman Helm oot o' here, tae. Find her a back room somewhere.'

The inspector clearly thought the job was beneath him, but since O'Malley clearly wanted a word with me on his own, there was no one else he could delegate the job to.

'Well done, lad,' O'Malley said. 'Ye just got there just in time. Did you see her put the bleach in yersel'?'

'Not personally, sir, but there's an entirely reliable witness who did.' I nodded in Mary's direction.

'Ye'd better introduce me, then,' O'Malley said.

'This is Sister Mary Maxwell-Hume, of the Sisters of Mary of the Sacred Cross.'

'A nun!' O'Malley said. 'How come I didnae notice a woman as nice-looking as youz, Sister?' He was about to offer his hand for Mary to shake when he stopped and took a step back. 'That's… an interesting dress, Sister. Dae yez always…?'

Mary smiled enigmatically. 'Our order believes in wearing only as much clothing as is necessary to maintain due modesty.'

A lascivious smile developed across Jack O'Malley's face. 'Well,' he said, 'the Lord works in mysterious ways.'

'Very true, Superintendent. That's what I keep trying to demonstrate to people.'

O'Malley chuckled, then asked me, 'Knox, do I get the impression that you two already knew each other?'

'Sister Mary's my piano teacher,' I explained.

'Piano teacher, yez say?' O'Malley hesitated, then put his head back and roared with laughter, causing many in the room to turn round and look at him. 'Well, I wisnae expecting that. And tell me, Sister, is that no' perfume…?'

'Chanel No.5,' I answered on Mary's behalf.

'Sae yez are an expert on perfume, are yez Knox? Interesting. Lipstick, too, it seems.' O'Malley turned back to Mary. 'Does your order allow you to wear lipstick, Sister?'

'We can only wear what preserves due modesty.'

The superintendent was being given the runaround, but he was enjoying it.

'Let's take that as a 'no' for the moment.' He turned to look at me intently.

'Well, Knox, what's the lipstick? Ye said it's the same on baith glasses. Can yez identify the lipstick at this distance?'

I crossed my fingers behind my back, praying that I'd remembered the answer correctly.

'It's Chanel, as well, as it happens,' I said. 'They make lipstick, too. That one is Rouge Allure Velvet, shade number 46.'

O'Malley raised his eyebrows in amusement. 'I'll take yer word for that, Knox.'

'P.C. Knox was even telling me that the shade had a name, Superintendent,' Mary said, although of course it was she who was the real expert on all the detail.

'Go on,' said O'Malley. 'Yez are gonnae tell me anyway.'

'*La Malicieuse*,' Mary said. "The malicious woman.' Rather appropriate, wouldn't you say? The answer was in the lipstick all along.'

COMPETITION TIME

'I think it's time you entered a piano competition, John.'

Perhaps I'm being overly modest when I say that my piano playing is excruciating: 'dreadfully poor', 'pretty awful' might be fairer assessments. Given the right piece, I can even reach the giddy heights of 'mediocre'. But no matter how much I try to dress it up, I am not a 'good' pianist. As my piano teacher, Mary Maxwell-Hume, never tires of telling me.

'Mary,' I said, 'forgive me doubting your judgement, but I really don't think my piano playing is ready to be let loose on the outside world. Somehow I don't see myself hammering into to that Tchaikovsky Piano Concerto thing.'

She shuddered. 'Oh, John, no, what a horrible thought! That's such an unpleasant piece… bang, bang, bang, bang… then the audience gets to fall asleep for 45 minutes.' She continued, 'But I'm not suggesting a competition open to the public.'

I must have looked even more confused than usual. Sister Mary Maxwell-Hume had that effect on me and, I suspect, on many others. All male.

'I have quite a lot of piano students, John. I wondered if they might all like to compete for a prize?'

'Are there any as bad as me?'

'They're all dreadful, John. You're the least bad. Don't you think it's a good idea?'

I tried to take in this non-compliment from the woman sitting at the other end of the sofa. Today she was wearing an elegant sapphire blue dress that stretched demurely all the way from her collar down to ankle length. With her shoes kicked off at the front door – she always insisted that I did the same – I knew exactly what she'd else she'd be wearing. Not that there was much room for doubt anyway: the dress stretched snugly over every last aspect of her figure. Of late, she'd taken to sitting just a fraction closer to me as well – which made me even more aware of her Chanel No.5, of course. But she and I very rarely made contact when we spoke casually.

At the piano stool, though, it was full-on. If she sat there beside me, either to demonstrate some point of technique or to play some duet, every possible point of contact was used – arms and shoulders brushed quite a bit, and our thighs and hips touched all the time. She liked to say that our duet playing would be more coupled if we ourselves we were more coupled. All these thoughts flashed through my mind as I took in the dress and what the dress barely concealed, while at the same time I tried to fix my gaze firmly on her face.

'You like it, John?'

Slightly flustered, I hesitated, then it slipped out.

'Stunning, Mary.'

A broad smile swept across her face. 'How wonderful, I'm so pleased you agree!'

'Agree with what?' I was still confused.

'That you should take part in my piano competition, of course,' she said. 'My, John… whatever were you referring to?' The smile became more complex: I could tell she was trying to look mystified, not very successfully.

Trapped, I conceded a little ground. Anything was a better than a confession.

'OK, Mary, tell me what you had in mind.'

Mary's smile returned to 'broad' status. 'Oh, John, I'm so pleased that you're keen to take part. It'll do your piano playing a power of good, you know – your technique and your confidence levels will leap forward. And of course each of us will get an independent assessment of your playing abilities.'

'Sorry, Mary, but exactly what am I going to have to do?'

'You'll have to give a recital. It'll be just like doing an exam, except that there's a prize for the best performance.'

The word 'exam' sent a cold shiver down my spine.

'Mary, I'm obliged to remind you that the piano exams I took as a boy were two of the most terrifying experiences I've ever had in my life.'

'Worse than confronting a bank robber, say?'

'Much worse. It's like facing a firing squad.'

'In that case it's good training for the dangers of being one of the emergency services. And it cleanses the soul, too,' she added. There were times, a lot of times, when I had to be reminded that Mary Maxwell-Hume was actually one of the Sisters of Mary of the Sacred Cross; briefly, she'd slipped into nun-mode. 'And at least you won't be alone in my competition.'

'You mean the other competitors?' I said. 'Well, I will be when I actually play, apart from the judges. Won't I?'

'No you won't. You're forgetting the audience.'

I had one of those moments when your life passes slowly before you.

'Aud...i....ence?'

'Naturally. People will come and listen to you perform – your supporters, talent-spotters and so on. We'll be selling tickets.'

Ah. That last four-word sentence had made everything clear. Mary Maxwell-Hume plus Scheme equals Money: one of the iron laws of mathematics. Straight away I could see a flaw.

'Mary, I gather that my role in this competition is to be

fed to the lions, Colosseum-style.'

'Rather a negative analogy, John, if I may so. But a very Christian way of looking at things, all the same.'

I ignored that. 'Who's going to pay good money to see and hear me play badly?'

'Lots of people. We'll sell tickets to all of your friends and relatives. And we'll hold a raffle. And sell programmes.'

'None of my relatives live anywhere nearby, and if any of my friends came, they'd not be friends with me ever again.'

'Come, come, John. You must do this. You must do it for the Sisters.'

'The Sisters? What do they have to do with it?'

'The event should be for charity, John. Prizes for the winners, sure, but we must raise money for good causes, too. Like the Sisters.'

'Sorry, Mary,' I said, firmly. 'I'm not going to make an idiot of myself for a curious order of nuns, only one of whom I've ever met.'

'In which case you must do it for me,' Mary's siren-like voice called to me. She took me by the hand – itself an unusual event – and led me to the piano. She signalled that I should sit down on the stool, then placed a score on the music stand – Satie's *Gymnopédie No. 1*.

'Play it, John. Play it for me.' I'd heard someone use those very words once before… yes, Ingrid Bergman in Casablanca. And I was no more able to resist than Sam, and he didn't have to put up with her follow-up line, 'I want an all-over massage with Eric Satie.'

I can't pretend it was perfect, but *Gymnopédie No. 1* is not an impossible piece to play and I duly pummelled Mary's body with it. She, on the other hand, viewed the piece differently. Just as I finished, I caught a glimpse of her caressing her own body in time to the music. I was a little surprised that my piano playing had any sense of 'time' at all.

I sat for a few seconds to wait for her to say something.

'Not bad, John. Not wonderful, but better than the others can manage. You could definitely play that in the competition.'

'What else do I have to do?'

Mary sat down on the stool beside me. 'Competitors will sight-read a completely new piece.'

'Sight-read!' I shouted, rather louder than I'd intended. 'Mary, that's not fair. Everyone hates sight-reading.'

'Indeed. But it's one of your strong points.'

'Eh?'

She backtracked a little. 'Perhaps 'strong' is not the word. But your sight-reading is a lot less 'weak' than everyone else's.'

'Really?'

'You never have to listen to Mr Morton. Or Mr Duggan. Or any of the others. Take my word for it, John.'

'Is that all I have to do? Sight-reading and Erik Satie?'

'No,' Mary said, 'there's one other element. Each pianist will play a piece for four hands.'

I looked at Mary as if she herself had four heads, then burst out laughing.

'Mary, I don't have four hands. Haven't you noticed? And I'm certain that even you don't have an extra pair tucked away under that dress.'

I thought it was funny – I'd no idea what she was talking about – but I'd forgotten that Mary Maxwell-Hume's sense of humour sometimes went AWOL, especially where music was concerned.

'You provide two of the hands, and another pianist provides the other two. Thankfully, you'll only have to sit on the left-hand side of the stool and play the easy bits.'

I don't know why I asked the next question. I knew the

answer already.

'Who plays the other half along with me?'

'Why me, of course,' she said. 'Who else?' She seemed quite bemused that I should have to ask.

'And will you play with the other competitors, too?'

'But of course, John. The conditions must be the same for everyone. And of course there will be a judging panel, of which I'll be one.' Then she added, 'But I have the utmost confidence that you'll emerge triumphant.'

Mary filled me in on some of the competition details. There would be an entry fee of £100, which I said seemed a lot: she insisted that there were 'considerable running costs' in organising such a tournament. Trinity Central Hall in the north of Edinburgh would be an ideal venue. No, she didn't know what the prize might be, but she hoped it would perhaps be £1000, depending on entries, the number of spectators who came, and uptake of the raffle tickets. I couldn't imagine many spectators coming to fill a hall that sat over a thousand. The judging panel was a surprise, though: three sisters from the Sisters of Mary of the Sacred Cross, of which she would naturally be one. But when I expressed my joy that I would finally meet some of her fellow nuns, she immediately cautioned me.

'John, please remember that these are nuns. They've given their lives to God and some of them have undertaken never to speak to any man. Our order respects that shyness, and they're allowed to remain apart from the outside world.'

'So I won't see them?' I said, curious.

'Oh yes, you'll see them, you'll be aware of them, but I'll be the only judge you'll probably speak to. I'll be the Chair of the Judging Panel.' Then Mary changed tack completely. 'Right now, let me sit on the piano stool beside you and we can try out playing a piece for four hands.'

The next eight weeks shot by. I was encouraged to come more often for (still free) lessons, while Mary Maxwell-Hume began to organise her piano competition. Posters advertising the event started to appear across the Trinity area. She told me that fourteen of her pupils, including me, had paid their fee and entered, although in the end that number dropped to ten. I learned that I would be playing something from Ravel's *Mother Goose Suite* along with Mary, a piece in five movements that ranged from simple to more tricky. Others would have to play from a selection of pieces by the Austrian composer Anton Diabelli. Competitors would know whether they were playing Ravel or Diabelli, but wouldn't know which movement they'd have to play – they would have to draw lots at the competition. That way the audience would get some fun as well, all at the poor pianists' expense. The entire show could easily have been entitled *Edinburgh's Got No Talent*.

I hadn't expected the seats to sell so well. Mary, it appeared, had contacts, and had sent two complimentary tickets to the Chief Constable along with a letter suggesting that my exploits as piano player would make great copy for the police newsletter and the local press. Chief Constable Grainger thought it was a great idea, promised to come, and insisted that some of his senior officers attend with their wives, too – doing so would be good for their career prospects, he hinted. The result was that I even received grumbling requests for tickets from Superintendent O'Malley and Inspector Plews, as well as several other more enthusiastic colleagues who saw the chance to cheer on their friend in a talent show. They also purchased well over three hundred raffle tickets at two pounds apiece, 'Proceeds towards the Sisters of Mary of the

Sacred Cross Emergency Rescue Fund'. Mary's other pupils managed to shift some tickets for the concert, raffle tickets too, but it was already clear that the bulk of the audience would be cheering for me. And 'cheering' was what they assured me that they would be doing: I was destined for a raucous evening.

Mary was delighted by the ticket sales, which eventually sold out ten days before the competition. She was less delighted by my piano playing.

'John, I'm concerned that you're going to let yourself down next Thursday evening. You should be better at *Mother Goose* than you are.'

'Some parts of it are easier than others,' I pleaded.

'Anyone can play the first movement,' she sniffed. 'But you'd be lucky to draw that. You have to prepare for the hardest pieces.' I was instructed to move along the piano stool a little to let her join me. 'I think it's time to attempt a concert performance. Let's see what you can do.'

Today, Mary was wearing one of her favourite scarlet dresses, but it seemed of an unusually thin, clinging material. As ever, it covered her completely from collar to ankle, while at the same time revealing everything. And she was very close to me. Had she not been a woman of God, I might even have suggested that she was snuggling her lower half against me. In order to create a little space for the upper half of her body, she was actually slightly sitting on me, not that Mary carried much weight at all.

Sensing my confusion, she said, 'I've told you before, John, in order to play a duet for four hands, we must play as a unit. We must be at one with one another.'

I didn't – couldn't – answer. I just wondered how much of her Chanel No.5 would cling to me. All that I could do was to close my mind, concentrate and play. To be fair, I have to acknowledge that Mary's 'four-hand method' encouraged more exact keeping of time, although she used a rather unusual metronome.

Once we'd ploughed through *Mother Goose*, Mary returned to her sofa to endure my latest rendition of *Gymnopédie No.1* – 'caress me with Satie, John' – then we moved on to the sight-reading exercises. Mary's chosen method was to provide me with a large folder containing sixty-four numbered pieces, then, she drew numbered ping-pong balls from a black plastic bag to decide which one I'd attempt. Long ago, I'd worked out that the pieces were graded, but in no particular order: this time, the numbers were 33, 61, 7 and 43. Piece 33 was easy, whereas pieces 7 and 61 were tricky. Piece 43 was brutally difficult.

Once it was all over, she gave her verdict: damning, as usual. Mary said that I appeared to be 'sight-reading the music like a blind man', had 'beaten her up' with the Satie rather than 'caressing her'; but she was pleased to say that *Mother Goose* was 'half good, half bad' – her part being the good bit, of course. To make up for it, I was instructed to play a very simple piece that I'd played many times before, her own *Study In A flat*, which she pronounced 'mediocre'. Then, suddenly, the lesson was over.

As she saw me to the door, I said to her, 'Mary, is this really a good idea?'

Mary looked horrified. 'Oh John, you must enter, you must. I so want you to win.'

'I think we both know that's rather unlikely,' I said.

'By the way,' she said, 'did you bring your £100 entry fee?'

I handed over five twenty-pound notes, freshly withdrawn from the cash machine on the way to her house. I could have said something about it being a large entry fee. I could have asked for a little more detail about the likely prizes. I could have asked how much she hoped to make for the Sisters of Mary of the Sacred Cross Emergency Rescue Fund, or for some details of that fund's likely beneficiaries. But I'd been getting free lessons for a while, to say nothing of the professional assistance she'd given me. I certainly seemed to be getting more from our association than she was.

And so I was committed: committed to making a fool of myself along with nine other men of varying ages, including 'Mr Morton' and 'Mr Duggan', whoever they were. For the next few days, I practised intensely and even signed up for extra lessons. Lacking the necessary talent, I knew it wouldn't help much, but I was desperate to feel that I was at least doing my best – not just for me, but for Mary, too.

Shortly before 7.00 p.m. on Thursday 9th July, I was trying to calm myself in the dressing-room of Trinity Central Hall. Sitting centre stage at one end of the hall sat a grand piano, like a French Revolutionary guillotine waiting to administer justice to each of its ten players. Seated out in the body of the hall were an awful lot of people waiting to see each execution in turn: a sell-out, in fact. That had me thinking, too. The manager of the hall was an old school friend of mine, and he mentioned that he'd let Mary have the hall for free 'because the Sisters were such a good cause'.

I'd already met the other competitors, including Mr Morton and Mr Duggan about whom I'd heard so much. Mr Morton was a small bald man with glasses, whom I'd assumed was perhaps a bank manager until he let it slip that he was actually a former airline pilot. Mr Duggan, it seemed, was some sort of surveyor. The other men were all older than me as well. A retired teacher called Brian seemed nice enough, and he was kind enough to pass on a few tips about dealing with nerves. By and large, though, the conversation covered the usual stuff – what everyone was playing, how they felt, and of course the weather. One thing I did pick up was that Mary was charging my fellow competitors – and charging a lot – for all of these extra lessons. It didn't seem a good idea to let on that mine were being given for free.

Out in the hall, on the other hand, the audience was anything but silent. Many of my colleagues had spent the period between the end of their shift in the Dragon Arms, a large bar in the Trinity area with a selection of excellent beers. I'd estimate that approximately four hundred of 'supporters' of mine had between them quaffed well over a thousand pints of beer, and they were making noise to match. When someone caught sight of me trying to get a sneak look, a huge cheer went up, followed by a wave of 'shhhh'. I felt embarrassed enough to apologise to Mary for my colleagues' behaviour.

'It's all right, John,' she surprised me by replying. 'They've each paid their ten pounds like everyone else. Don't worry, it's our job – your job – to win their respect. Which you will.' She said it with such authority that I believed her, although I'd no idea why.

On the stroke of seven o'clock Mary Maxwell-Hume strode onto the centre of the stage. She began by welcoming everyone, and thanking them for supporting the Sisters' Emergency Relief Fund. She went on to explain the format of the competition – sight-reading, then playing a four-hand piece, then finally each competitor would get a chance to play one 'showcase' piece of their own choosing.

Then she pointed towards the other two judges on the panel. I'd spotted them in position before, tucked away in a dark corner of the hall, and was rather taken aback that they were both in full red nun's habit. No part of their face could be seen, they sat stock still, although I was interested that each wore Chanel No.5 – it was obvious to anywhere near the front of the hall. Mary explained that these were 'silent order' nuns, barred from communicating with anyone outside their own order, and that she, Mary, would be the Chair of the panel. Then she surprised everyone by announcing that consideration would be given to audience appreciation at the end of each piece, so that listeners were encouraged to clap and encourage performers.

Then it was showtime.

First to the stage was a middle-aged taxi-driver called Rab. Rab went across to Mary, drew a ping-pong ball out of a black cloth bag, then walked nervously across to sit at the piano. He turned to the page allocated by the number, and began. I'd like to say he was good, but even I would have been ashamed. Eventually he stumbled to the end, stood up and left to a sympathetic round of applause.

They weren't all as bad as Rab, but none of the next four players were convincing. Brian played not badly, but his piece was definitely one of the easier ones.

Then it was my turn. I actually received a couple of encouraging cries from my drunken support, which in truth didn't settle my nerves one little bit. As I went across to Mary, who mouthed 'God is with you, John' at me, drew out number 25, and made my way to the piano. I turned to the piece on the folder sitting on the piano.

It took me a moment to get my bearings. There, facing me, was *Study in A Flat* by Mary Maxwell-Hume, that piece I played every lesson and I could have sworn I'd never seen in the file before. Too confused to question anything, I just got on with it – not perfectly, of course, but to the audience it must have sounded magnificent by comparison with what had gone before. At the end, I stood up and even took a discreet bow of the head as the audience whooped and hollered.

Once the other players' turns had come and gone, Mary consulted the other two judges on the panel. Then she stepped forwards to address the audience.

'I hope you enjoyed that. Sight-reading is very difficult and nerve-racking for the players, and they've each tried their best.' The audience began to applaud, and she raised a hand to silence them again. 'I won't tell you all of the scores just now, but I will say that Mr Lennox Washington is in third place with five points, Mr Brian Reid is in second with six points, but our leader is Mr John Knox with a perfect ten points.'

This time she allowed the audience to get the cheering out of their system.

'Next,' she said, when the noise had subsided, 'we move on to the point where I play a piece alongside each competitor in turn.' She explained that the ten of us would work our way through five Diabelli pieces, then we would move on to Ravel's *Mother Goose Suite*. The audience would therefore hear each of the pieces right through, but played in installments by each of us. This time she suggested that the audience stay silent between movements, and that she'd bring us each forward individually at the end. Amazingly, I drew the easiest piece, the opening *Pavane* from *Mother Goose*. I was therefore sixth on stage, after the Diabelli.

None of the other pianists coped well with Mary sitting beside them. When my chance came, though, Mary did exactly what I was used to, in full body-contact below the waist, helping me keep the beat: the Pavane went pretty well. At the end of the round, I got easily the biggest cheer, and once Mary had consulted her red-habited colleagues, she addressed the audience again.

'Ladies and gentlemen, thank you for your help. The

panel have once again listened to you and thank you for judgement. For the last round, the performance,' – she stressed its significance – 'the players will play in reverse order of where they stand in the scoring.' Then she went on to announce the positions, working her way up from tenth all the way to first, finishing with, '...and last to play, currently leading by six points, is... John Knox!'

Once again, the audience was allowed to let a thousand pints of beer make a little more noise.

At last, each of us was allowed to play something that we knew and had prepared. Mr Morton played something called *Sad Story* by Maconchy, which indeed sounded very sad; Rab managed to play a straightforward piece by an American composer called Bruce Levine; and Brian Reid played something by the English composer James Hook. Each in turn was politely applauded. Then it was my turn.

I'd practised so much I didn't really need the music, but I took it with me anyway. Once again there were a few drunken shouts of encouragement from colleagues, but the hall fell into respectful silence as I began to play the Satie. It wasn't great, but Mary was right, stage performances often bring out the best in musicians. There's the faintest hesitation in *Gymnopédie No.1* – no more than a dramatic pause – before the second part starts, and when I snatched a glance across to Mary she was... caressing herself. It was easier to play from there on with my eyes closed, which must have looked as though I was dreaming along with the music blissfully. I was only trying to prevent being distracted. The audience loved it: for once, someone was actually playing a piece that it recognised. I bowed briefly, and mercifully it was all over.

Mary went across to the corner where her two fellow sisters sat utterly impassively. There was a brief discussion, she wrote down a few notes, then she returned to the centre of the stage holding a few pieces of card and some envelopes.

'Ladies and gentlemen,' she said, 'thank you all once again for coming to support us. I hope you've all enjoyed yourselves, and I think you'll agree that all ten of our competitors have done very well.' That triggered the mandatory round of applause. 'And now you'll want to hear the results. In third place… is David Mackay.'

David Mackay stepped forward to receive an envelope. He didn't know that there was a third prize.

'In second place… Brian Reid.'

Brian, too, stepped forward to receive an unexpected prize.

'And the winner is… John Knox.'

It's difficult to describe the feeling when an audience cheers at the sound of your name; certainly an awful lot of people seemed to be very happy as I, too, collected an envelope. Only one person seemed not to share their joy: Inspector Maximilian Plews. Plews had a face like thunder. To his left, his wife was shaking her head in despair while to his right Superintendent Jack O'Malley seemed to find something incredibly funny. The thousand-pint beer group began to sing 'For he's a jolly good fellow' at the top of their collective voices until eventually Mary called a halt.

'Ladies and gentlemen, as a token of appreciation for their participation, each of the other competitors will receive a small prize as well.' The delight in Mr Morton's eyes was particularly nice to see.

Mary continued. 'Please can you also show your appreciation for the other two members of the judging panel?' There was polite applause for the two red-hooded silent Sisters, who remained resolutely still and unresponsive.

Just in time, I remembered to step forward and thank Mary for organising the competition.

'Thank you, John,' she said, then turning to the audience continued, saying, 'And thank you all for coming to support us, and I wish you all a safe journey home. Perhaps we can repeat this next year? In the meantime, please put your hands together for our champion, John Knox.'

The evening had finally come to an end. Superintendent O'Malley came forward to congratulate me, but he was still laughing.

'Well done, Knox lad. Easily the best man won. Maybe no' done yer promotion prospects much good, mind.'

'I dinna – don't understand, sir.'

'The Inspector slightly underestimated your abilities on the piano. He was prepared to bet £10 wi' anyone around that you couldnae win.'

'Oh dear,' I said. 'Did a lot of people take him up on it?'

'Well, tae begin wi', everyone whae's here. Plus the secretarial staff, and the cleaners, and…' He thought for a moment. 'I reckon he's lost over two thousand pounds.'

'Ouch. Did you take him on?'

'Aye, of course.'

'How were you so sure?' I asked, although I had my suspicions.

'A wee burd tipped me off,' O'Malley said. Then his mind seemed to wander. 'Nice lookin' wumman, yon nun…' He turned back to me. 'Anyway, well done again, Knox. Ye've made ma week.'

My prize was £1000, Brian Reid had won £500 and David Mackay's third prize was £200. The others had each had their £100 entry fee returned. Everyone else was buzzing with excitement, but it was obvious that there was more to all of this than met the eye. I wanted to help tidy up, but Mary refused to let me do so – she insisted on leaving it till the next day. Instead, she just asked for a lift home immediately.

'What about the other Sisters?' I asked.

'They'll make their own way home,' she said. 'They're forbidden to talk to you or look at you.'

'They don't exist, Mary. There's nobody under those habits.'

She looked at me, shocked. Then she said, 'Is it that obvious?'

I laughed. 'Only to me, Mary. I know you better than the others. And there was more than one bag of ping-pong balls, wasn't there? One for all the other competitors, and my one was full of balls marked 25. Yes?'

She shrugged her shoulders.

'And I'm guessing that something similar gave me the easiest piece in the *Mother Goose Suite*.'

'Must you be a policeman all the time, John?' I sensed a little bitterness in her voice. 'I thought you'd be grateful.'

'I like winning fair and square.'

'You did win fair and square, John. You're by far the best of my pupils. No one else gets close to playing Satie the way you do. I actually enjoy listening to you. And you have got a feel for the piano. That contact in the four-hand pieces… it's a two-way thing. I move with your rhythm, too. The piano is such a sensuous instrument, you know.'

'I know,' I said quietly. 'You've taught me that. By the way, thanks for the prizemoney. Can I ask you a question?'

'Go on.'

'How will the money raised for the Sisters' Emergency Fund get used?'

Her hesitation told me that I was close to crossing the line, and I made a mental note to be more careful in future.

'John, there are a lot of necessary expenses. There was the hire of the hall for a start.'

As she said it, I remembered my old school friend, the hall manager.

'And I have expenses of my own. Standards to maintain,' she added, smoothing her dress.

'Of course,' I conceded. 'There probably won't be much left over.' From ticket sales, the raffle and programme sales, only a few thousand, I thought inwardly.

Not my business. Not worth losing a good friendship over.

CHRISTMAS

'What are you doing for Christmas, Mary?'

'I might spend it with the Sisters,' Mary Maxwell-Hume said.

'Will lots of the Sisters be around?' I asked. We were sitting in my Smart panda car. Mary had once again inveigled a lift to the shops, this time to look at a couple of new dresses. She always went to the same department store, Murrays in Princes Street, who could provide dresses made to fit her exact shape perfectly. This time, she said, she was looking at a couple of warmer dresses for the winter, in shades of red, naturally.

'Some of them,' Mary said, rather vaguely. She tended to look away from me when when something was troubling her, and occasionally I wondered if she was trying to hide a tear from me. I didn't pry, though. Mary never offered me anything of her private life at all.

'How about you, John?' she said, turning round after a while to look at me with a smile that might just have been switched on as she did so. 'Do you have family?'

'Yes and no,' I said.

'Oh, I do like 'yes and no' answers, John. I need to know more.' I had the impression that she was shifting the conversation away from herself.

'Yes, I do have family,' I began. 'But they all live in Australia. Melbourne, to be exact.' I explained that I had an older brother and sister, each of whom had emigrated and had families. My parents realised that they if they were going to see their grandchildren, they'd have to emigrate before they were too old, before the Australian government saw them as a potential burden and refused to let them in.

'So you were left behind?'

'I suppose so. There's Skype. We keep in touch that way.'

'It's not the same, is it?' she said. 'You need to touch and feel your loved ones as well as see them on a computer screen or through a loudspeaker. You even need to smell them,' she added as she dabbed on a little more Chanel No.5 using the little atomiser she stored in my car.

'I suspect that if my parents could smell me now I'd have the scent of Chanel all over me,' I chuckled.

'There's worse. Anyway, what will you do at Christmas?'

'I don't know. I usually volunteer to work over Christmas. New Year, too. It gives the ones with families the chance to be together, and I can build up lots of overtime. Not this year, though.'

'Why not?'

'There's a demand for the overtime. A couple of guys have debt problems, and there are two new Asian PCs, both Muslims who really don't much care about Christmas. The ovetime has to be shared around, it seems.'

'How strange.'

'So I'll be glued to whatever's on television, I suppose. Eating some sort of TV dinner. The supermarkets usually have a great range of stuff for sad people like me.'

'You're not 'sad', John. Just alone.'

After a moment's hesitation, I summoned up some courage. 'Are you alone, Mary?'

She looked away again. 'I'm never alone, John. I have God.'

'You know what I mean. Will you have any human company for Christmas?'

'I told you, I have the Sisters. I'll spend it with whoever is around.'

'Except that none of the Sisters will be around for Christmas, will they?'

She didn't answer. Instead, I heard her breathing in deeply. Then she said, a hint of bitterness in her voice, 'You tell me, John, you seem to be the detective around here.' Still, she refused to look at me. But the darkness allowed me a glimpse of redness in her eyes as they reflected in the car window.

Once again I broke the silence. 'We seem to be a right pair, you and I. I'd invite you for Christmas myself but you've seen my flat. You couldn't swing a cat in it, far less make Christmas dinner.'

'It's a nice flat, John. And thank you for the thought, anyway. It was very generous. But I might not be great company anyway, to be honest.' I waited for her to continue, but instead she simply said, 'Thank you for the lift, John. Could you come back and collect me again in an hour?'

As she opened the door to get out, I wondered, not for the first time, how this woman had turned me from police constable into her personal chauffeur. And, as demanded, I was there again to collect her exactly sixty minutes later.

'Success, Mary?' I asked, as got in. 'Find what you were looking for?'

'I think so,' she said. 'Murrays is such a reliable shop. I'm fortunate, my measurements don't change all that much from month to month, so it's not hard for them to make dresses that fit me. I just order them and they deliver.'

'You never try anything in the shop on for size?'

'Shop dresses on the rails never fit correctly. I set high standards.'

I smiled. 'I've noticed.' I was concentrating on the traffic and it just slipped out.

In the passenger seat, I could see slowly turning to smile at me. 'You have?'

'In everything,' I said, hoping that Mary would accept that.

'I'm so glad you think so,' she said, but out of the corner of my eye I could see the smile continue to play on her lips as we drove along. I decided to try and stay focused on the road before I got into any more hot water, so the rest of our journey was largely silent until we turned into the street where she lived. It had started to rain and I was concerned that her dress would get wet – goodness knows how she handled the winter temperatures – so I offered to pop into her house and fetch an umbrella. She jumped at the offer, but when I returned to the car, she was already getting out.

'Thank you, John. That was very chivalrous of you.'

'I'm not sure I'm allowed to lay my uniform across a puddle to stop you getting your feet wet,' I joked.

'Pity,' she said. I wondered if this was her turn to slip up, but then she added simply, 'How times have changed. Thank you again, and I'll see you soon.'

'No doubt. Bye, Mary,' I said, as she closed the passenger door.

I had to do a three-point turn to get the car out of Mary's narrow street. As I started to go back past Mary's house in the other direction, I was surprised to see her still in the roadway. She tapped on my window and I wound it down.

'Perhaps you might come to my house?'

'Christmas?'

'It's just a thought.'

I didn't have to think very long. The thought of spending another Christmas on my own really didn't appeal very much. I was happy enough to work at Christmas, but I just hadn't been prepared to admit that when I came off shift, I was still pretty lonely.

'I'd love to, Mary. Thank you for inviting me.'

A few days later Mary was back in the Smart panda car.

'Good morning, Mary,' I said. 'Where to, today? Christmas shopping?'

'No,' she said. 'I need to go to Murrays again.' Mary rarely said 'please' in these situations; she seemed to regard my transportation service as an entitlement, something she paid taxes for. Perhaps she was right.

I realised that Mary was probably going to collect the dresses she'd ordered earlier in the week on our previous visit. Today, the temperature was barely above freezing and she had chosen to wear a warm woollen dress and stylish shoes, but as usual it was entirely obvious that those were the only three items of clothing she was wearing. Naturally, I already knew that the Sisters of Mary of the Sacred Cross insisted that members of the Order wear 'only as much clothing as was necessary to preserve due modesty.'

'How do you manage in this cold weather?' I asked her.

'We train our bodies to adapt, John,' she explained. 'You can, you know. People live in very hot climates, and the Finnish roll around in snow after a sauna.'

'Can you do that? The sauna thing, I mean?'

She hesitated, then smiled. 'I have done, a few times. I found it quite exhilarating, actually.' She looked at me, clearly amused. 'Does the thought appeal to you?'

Mary loved confusing me with these dual-meaning questions. Now it was my turn to take my time and be careful.

'I don't really fancy rolling around naked in snow, no,' I said.

Mary smiled, but said nothing. I felt it might be a good

idea to change the conversation to a safer topic.

'Is that invitation to Christmas at your house still open?'

She looked alarmed. 'Oh yes, John, of course it is! I'd be so disappointed if you couldn't come now.'

'Don't worry, I'd love to come. I just wanted to check.'

We discussed what we might eat. She loved the traditions of Christmas, she said, which meant turkey, with all the trimmings, was essential; but we agreed that we really couldn't justify an entire bird for just two people. Something from a supermarket would have to do. Chippolata sausages, stuffing, vegetables, cranberry sauce and any other items could come from the same source. For a starter, I offered to bring some smoked salmon from my favourite fishmonger. We discussed pudding, but she said she wanted to surprise me.

There was another subject I needed to bring up.

'Mary, I'd like to give you a present. But apart from Chanel No.5, I can't think of anything I could possibly buy you that would be of any use.'

'You don't need to give me a present, John.'

'I know I don't need to, Mary. But I'd like to.'

'Really, you don't need to give me anything.'

'Please give me a clue. I can hardly buy you a dress.'

'No,' she agreed. 'Honestly, anything will do. But don't spend a lot of money, please. It's your company that I'm looking forward to having.'

'That's a nice thing to say.'

'I mean it. If we're talking presents, is there anything you yourself would like?'

I'd thought about this. Given that Mary was unlikely to pay for many of the things she supposedly 'bought' in shops, I didn't want to have to worry about receiving stolen goods. 'Well… there is, actually.'

She looked at me anxiously. 'Well?'

'I know you can make CDs on that computer of yours – the one that you use to print out music. I'd love a recording of you playing some lovely music on the piano.'

I could see from her surprise and joy that I'd asked for something she felt was appropriate.

'We'll see,' she said.

At work, my days were full, as those who weren't due to work on Christmas Day naturally had work shifts on either side. Nevertheless Mary and I still managed to fit in a joint visit to Marks and Spencer to collect the turkey and trimmings that we needed – she could have done it on her own, but of course I was the chauffeur anyway. Needless to say, another visit to Murrays was required; this time Mary emerged with something in one of those large upmarket paper carrier bags with string handles. Collecting the smoked salmon and a few other small items had to wait until Christmas Eve.

Mary had suggested that I come over around three in the afternoon on Christmas Day. It was a lovely bright cold day and I'd decided to walk across from my flat, a distance of about three miles that would take an hour. In fact it took slightly less time, but I thought it would be rude to arrive early so I stood at the end of the street for seven or eight minutes before making my way along to her house. When I arrived, the front door was open.

'Just come in, John,' a voice called out. 'I'm through in the kitchen.'

When I found her, she was standing with her back to me, preparing some vegetables and a little salad.

'The front door was open,' I said, rather needlessly. 'But I presume you knew that.'

'You should have just come in. I saw you standing on the corner – waiting until three, I presume?'

'I was taught that it's rude to be early – you might not be quite ready.'

'Still not fully dressed, you mean? Hardly.' Mary still hadn't once turned around to face me. 'Well, for the future, I don't mind if you come early. It makes the most of the evening. Merry Christmas, by the way,' she added.

'Merry Christmas,' I said to the back. She was wearing yet another new dress, red, clinging to every crevice and outpost of her figure. Even from a distance, I could see that the dress had tiny white pinstripes running vertically its entire length from collar to ankle.

'Merry Christmas,' I said back, depositing my carrier bag on the kitchen table. In addition to the smoked salmon, I'd brought some cashew nuts and olives as well as a bottle of champagne and an expensive bottle of French red wine: it was Christmas, after all.

Mary glanced back at the table, but not at me. 'My, John, are you planning on getting me drunk?'

'Not at all, Mary. Just offering you a little choice.'

'We'll see.'

Eventually, the vegetable preparation complete, she turned around, smiled and said, 'There's actually some champagne in the fridge. Shall we?' It was the first time she'd actually looked at me.

I followed her through to her living room, carrying my olives, which she thought were a useful addition to our other canapés. We sat on her two sofas facing each other across a coffee table, an even more formal arrangement than usual. She approved of my olives; I complimented her little tapenades selection. We could have passed for new fumbling romantic acquaintances, except that she was old enough to be my mother and was actually my piano teacher. And a nun, of course. She had some soft solo piano music playing in the background: something baroque, perhaps even Bach or Scarlatti.

In time we ate, facing each other across her dining table, although admittedly she'd shortened it so that it was actually square. The salmon was excellent, she declared, superior to the fish available near her. We ate the TV dinner version of turkey and all the trimmings, which were far better than either of us could have expected. We certainly drank more than I'd expected, and Mary didn't seem affected at all.

'I need a rest,' I confessed, as she tidied away the turkey plates. 'In fact, I'd really like to wash those, if you'd let me. It would help all that food I've eaten settle a little.'

'That's really my job, John. But if you like, we can do them together.'

And so, mid-meal, we actually washed, dried and put away all the cutlery, dishes and pans that we'd used so far. I washed, she did everything else, although of course we put whatever we could into the dishwaher. But perhaps it was the ordinariness of housework that finally relaxed us. We chatted about the piano competition she'd recently organised, about my work, and about one or two of her favourite pianists. Then it was back to food.

'You said you had a surprise for pudding. Are you going to let me into the secret?'

She smiled quietly. 'No. You'll find out in due course. But I can tell you that it's a favourite of mine. Are you ready yet?'

'OK,' I said, 'bring it on.'

'You'll need to go back through to the dining room. This is my surprise, John.' All this time, we'd been standing in the kitchen, always a much more relaxed part of any house.

Five minutes later, she brought a large – very large – sundae through, which appeared to be a cross between a traditional trifle and a knickerbocker glory. It actually took two hands to carry it, and I was a little intimidated.

'Em... I can't eat all of this myself, Mary,' I said.

From somewhere about her person, she produced two long spoons, pulled her chair round beside mine, and announced, 'To share.'

And then, for five minutes, not much more, we silently shared the mix of ice creams, strawberries, raspberries, and champagne-soaked sponge, even feeding each other like teenagers on a date.

'I haven't had the chance to do that for years,' Mary said finally. 'Thank you, John.'

'It was your idea, Mary. I'm the one who should be doing the thanking.' But I sensed an opportunity. 'Have you had much chance to share puddings in the past?'

She sighed. 'A long time ago.'

'Can you tell me about him?' As an afterthought, I added, 'I'm assuming it was a 'him'.'

She smiled slightly. 'Yes, John. A 'him'. My husband, Douglas Maxwell-Hume. Perhaps we might go back to the living room to the comfortable chairs. I'm actually quite uncomfortable with all that eating. I'm very warm, too.'

As we entered the living room, she suddenly shocked me with a request.

'Will you help me, John? I need to be more at ease if I'm to talk about my past.'

'Of course. What can I do for you?'

'I can feel my waistline in this dress, and it feels tight. Would you help me loosen it? It has a zip at the back. The long delicate zips are often a bit of struggle, and I simply can't be bothered with the effort tonight.'

'You wear very neat dresses,' I said, as I started to examine the dress. 'Don't you sometimes wish you could relax a bit?'

'I can relax here. But one must maintain standards in

public.' Then she asked again, 'Can you manage?'

I'd seen men help women undo dress zips in old movies, and I half-expected it to be something similar. Mary's zip was well concealed and extremely fine – I could see why she wanted assistance – but this zip was also incredibly long. I started to work it downwards, before stopping around the small of her back.

'Is that far enough?'

'Is that as far as it goes?'

'No, it goes quite a bit further.'

'Would you mind?'

Slowly, I worked the zip down, waiting for Mary to tell me to stop; but she didn't, even when the zip passed her waist and the dress started to move outwards again. By the time I was done, I had established that she was definitely wearing nothing underneath. Not that her underwear status was news. Amazingly, the dress continued to cling to every part of her body. Then she sat down, this time alongside me, and for the first time she subtly loosened the dress's grip on her, which allowed Mary to place her back directly against the cool leather. She closed her eyes and gave a sigh of relief.

Then she told me everything. She was an only child. Her mother had died in childbirth giving birth to Mary herself, and her father had been forced to depend on assistance from the extended family for childcare. She'd spent a lot of time with her Uncle Leonard and family. Leonard had routinely abused her as a child. She'd reported it, but somehow Leonard managed to shift the blame on to her own father. Leonard's own two sons were key witnesses: they gave their father consistent alibis for every event, and the police and social workers couldn't believe that children so young could lie so effectively. They also managed to convince the social workers that they themselves had been the victim of Mary's father. Her father was jailed, and just a few months later he committed suicide in prison. She never saw him again. Worse still, she now felt responsible for the deaths of each of her parents.

Mary herself had been taken into foster care, a hideous experience that had messed up her education. Her only remaining talent had been playing the piano, so she'd gone to music college and trained as a professional. There, she'd met Douglas, a violin player, one thing had led to another and they'd ended up getting married three years later. It had all been very happy until Douglas had one day been found dead, having consumed an enormous number of sleeping pills. Unknown to Mary, he'd run up huge casino debts and couldn't take any more. Mary was left with the house they lived in, but lost everything else, even their car – Mary, it transpired, had a valid driving licence.

Devastated, she'd thrown herself into teaching the piano. And while she'd loved her husband dearly, her experience of men in general hadn't encouraged her to get involved again. In her own words, men were rather a 'sub-species'. She hadn't volunteered any further information about the Sisters of Mary of the Sacred Cross, and I didn't think I'd learn anything by asking.

'You've rather raised my hopes for the male gender, John,' she said. 'I hope you're not going to let me down, too.'

'I can only do my best, Mary.'

She said nothing for a long time, then said, 'I wish I were twenty-five years younger.'

I'd no idea how to respond. I found Mary exceptionally attractive, but she was old enough to be my mother. I think my silence unnerved her.

'I'm sorry, John,' she said. 'I've embarrassed you. Please forget I said that.'

This time I was able to answer. 'No, I won't. I'm flattered. In lots of ways I wish I were twenty-five years older. But I don't want to wish my life away.'

'Quite right, John. I've frittered decades of my life away. Don't make the same mistake.'

I took a deep breath. 'A very large part of me would actually like you to seduce me. But that would spoil everything, wouldn't it?'

She raised her eyebrows. 'Now it's my turn to be flattered. You'd be very welcome to stay the night. But you're right, it would spoil everything.

'Anyway,' she continued, 'this won't last for ever. One day you'll no longer be a police constable, you'll be promoted to very high levels. You'll not need any help from me then. You have a lot of talent, John, I can tell that. You don't let things fluster you, and you have compassion, and you have considerable detective skills of your own. You ask the right questions in a nice way.'

'I'll still need piano lessons,' I pointed out.

'I hope so.'

I felt the conversation was getting a little depressing, so I said it was nice that she'd kept her husband's name to preserve his memory.

'Oh, goodness me, no, John. That wasn't the reason at all. I was simply delighted to get rid of my real name.'

'Which was?'

'I was born Mary Madeleine Scarlett Plews.'

To say that I was stunned would be an understatement.

'Are you…?'

'Theodore and Maximilian are actually my cousins, yes. It was their father who abused me. Physically, psychologically, and, yes, sexually. Teddy and Max gave evidence against my father. I might be a nun, John, but I lost my innocence a long time ago.'

'Jesus,' I said.

'Jesus really did help me, John. It isn't an act.' I was about to apologise, but she stopped me. 'After all I've seen in my life, it takes a lot more than a word or two to offend me. I'm quite worldly, I think.'

'I don't doubt that.' I studied the woman sitting beside me. Her eyes were still closed, and her slightly loosened dress seemed to have relaxed her a little. 'Don't the Plews brothers know who you are?'

'I was only thirteen when I was taken away. I was a fat spotty teenager with glasses – I had a squint that needed correcting.'

I had to chuckle. 'That's a little hard to imagine, Mary. The ugly duckling who turned into a beautiful swan.'

Now, finally, she opened her eyes and turned to look at me.

'Why, John, that's a lovely thing to say,' she said, with the widest smile I'd seen in a long time. She reached across to squeeze my hand, an extraordinarily tender moment, then she got up to cross the room. Realising that I was looking away to avoid gazing at 'that back', she quietly said without looking back, 'It's all right, John, I'm perfectly happy to let you look. I feel safe with you. I haven't felt this safe with a man for a long time. Not since Douglas.'

'Thank you,' I said. 'Now it's your turn to say a nice thing.'

She opened a drawer. 'I have a present for you.'

She handed over a CD. 'It's what you asked for, a recording of me playing the piano. It was playing earlier.'

'It was beautiful. What was it?'

'Bach. The *Two-Part And Three-Part Inventions*. You might be able to play some of them yourself,' she said, and out of nowhere she produced a hardback copy of the complete sheet music. 'I wasn't sure if you'd like it. The receipt's inside.'

'It's perfect,' I said, genuinely thrilled. 'Thank you. You can teach me to play them all. And I have a present for you, too.' I went through to the kitchen, brought back the plastic carrier bag, and handed over two wrapped presents. She opened up the first, clearly a book: *A Visual History of Chanel*, a coffee-table book really, full of posters, photographs of Chanel products through the ages, and photographs of Coco Chanel and some of her consorts. Inside, I'd written 'To Mary, Happy Christmas, with love from John x'.

It wasn't hard to guess what the other gift, a box, contained.

'Thank you, John. You're very generous,' she said quietly, as she opened the Chanel No.5. Then, suddenly, there were tears in her eyes.

'Mary, what's wrong?'

'This might be the first Christmas present I've received in… perhaps twenty years.'

'No! Surely not – but that's awful, Mary.' I handed her a tissue.

'It's only Christmas,' she said, dabbing her eyes. 'Christmas shouldn't be about presents.'

'It should be about giving presents, Mary.'

'Well, I've not had anyone to give presents to either.'

I reached across. 'Can I hold you, Mary? Is that OK?'

With a snuffle, she simply nodded. There was no way of avoiding that back again, and this time I gently massaged it.

'Pretend I'm playing the Satie,' I joked. It didn't work.

'John,' she said eventually, 'I need to tell you something.'

I didn't like the sound of what might be coming.

'It's about how I acquire things,' she said. Now I was very concerned.

I took a deep breath. 'I think you're a very moral woman,

Mary.' I was thinking of her victims, of course: deserving cases, all of them.

She nuzzled in to me. 'Do I deserve your kindness, John? I doubt it.'

'Just tell me what the problem is,' I said, quietly.

'The receipt's not there in case you want to exchange the present,' she said. 'You'd never take it back to the shop – I know you're far too polite to do that. It's because I felt that I needed to prove to you that I hadn't stolen it to give it you. I'm so ashamed.'

'It really hadn't crossed my mind, Mary,' I said, honestly. Then a thought occurred to me. 'Would you write a message in the music for me?'

She stretched forwards for a pen that was lying on the coffee table and wrote, 'Happy Christmas to my good friend John, with all my love, Mary xx'.

'I'll cherish this, Mary,' I said. 'And I'll try to do the music justice.'

'I'll look forward to that.'

We sat for a while longer saying nothing, while I returned to gently massaging her back.

'Is this still all right, Mary?'

'It's lovely. I wish you could stay. Even if it were only in my spare room.'

I considered that for a minute, then said, 'I suppose if I stayed over in your spare room, we could have a little more wine.'

'We could. I've even got a spare toothbrush you could use.'

'Let's do that, then. I'll go and fetch the wine in a little while.' I was still massaging her back, which I was in no hurry to interrupt. Then I added, 'Only the spare room, though.'

She straightened up to face me, which had the side-effect

of edging my hand a good deal lower down her back.

'Please don't stop, it's lovely,' she whispered. Then she kissed me, this woman more than twice my age, a long, lingering, sensuous kiss, before drawing away slightly. At that point she could have done anything with me, and she knew it. I wanted her, she wanted me.

'The spare room it is,' she sighed. 'Such a waste. Right place, wrong time.'

'Right place, wrong time.' I kissed her again. 'Sadly.'

THE END

THE PIANO EXAM

'Hello?'

'Is Mary Maxwell-Hume there?'

'Speaking. How can I help you?' The voice at the other end of the line had an English accent, educated, certainly not working class.

'Do you give piano lessons?'

'That rather depends. Who are the lessons for?'

'Me.'

'And you are? I'm sorry I didn't catch your name.'

'I'm sorry. I should've introduced myself. My name's Brian Reid and I'm looking for a couple of piano lessons.'

'Just two? It usually takes a little longer than that,' the voice replied drily.

A good start, I thought. This woman did sardonic, it seemed. Don't encourage her, I thought inwardly. 'I was given your name by a friend. I was hoping you might be able to help me.'

'Which friend?' the voice asked.

'Joe Mackay.' I wanted to call him 'Little' Joe Mackay because that was what his brother – and my best man – always called him, but I managed to stop myself.

'You mean that pathetic ironmonger with the shop in Morningside?'

I didn't know how to reply to that. Joe did indeed have an ironmongery shop at the foot of Morningside Road in Edinburgh's Southside, but I didn't normally like to acknowledge that he was 'pathetic' to perfect strangers. Actually, he was pretty pathetic, but I decided not to admit it for the moment.

'You remember Joe?'

'I remember Joseph Mackay, yes. Good address, Merchiston Terrace, as I recall.'

'That's the one.'

'Far too heavy on the left hand. No sense of rhythm on the right.'

This was alarming. Did she discuss all of her pupils with perfect strangers?

'Do you discuss all of your pupils with perfect strangers?' I asked.

'Only the execrable ones. But I succeeded with Joseph.'

'You did?'

'I persuaded him to sell his piano. He had a Bechstein Grand which belonged in better hands. Advised him to try another instrument.'

'Such as?'

'A sat-nav. Any noise it makes is beyond his control.'

Wow. To think that this woman was recommended to me by Joe Mackay himself. I needed to update her, however.

'Joe only partially followed your advice,' I informed her.

'Oh?' It came out as a low growl.

'He sold his Bechstein, but he bought a guitar instead.'

'Not a sat-nav?'

'He had one already, as it happened. In his VW Passat. Although I've never seen him use it, now that I think about it.' I paused for a moment, then added, 'Perhaps he can't get it in tune.' It was meant to be a joke, trying to lighten the conversation.

'I don't suppose he *was* able to tune a sat-nav,' the woman suggested to me. She went on. 'Please tell me it's not one of those awful electric guitar things he's bought. They're so *crude* and *indelicate*.'

'Indeed it is, Ms. Maxwell-Hume.'

'With a stupidly loud amplifier?' She was pleading for a good answer.

'Afraid so.'

'In which case the whole world will hear how unmusical he actually is. Perhaps I should have encouraged him more in his piano playing. At least he didn't have one of those awful electric keyboard things.' Oh dear, I thought, but that could wait a while.

'I've never heard Joe, either on the piano or on guitar,' I told her. 'He might be better than me.'

'That would be good for his ego. He'd then only be the second-worst musician I've ever heard. However, I'm sure you didn't call me to discuss Joseph. You would like me to give you two piano lessons?'

'I didn't *literally* mean two. But I don't need too many.'

'I'll be the judge of that,' Mary Maxwell-Hume replied down the phone. Ouch. 'What are your aims, Mr. Reid?'

Now this was one I was ready for, because I happened to be a teacher, a depute headteacher in fact, so I knew all about 'aims and objectives'. Aims and objectives are things you claim to have thought about before you start, are working towards, and are usually far removed from where you end up.

'I'd like to pass a piano exam,' I told her. 'Grade Three.'

'Why Grade Three?' Mary Maxwell-Hume asked.

'Well… Actually, I'm not sure why I'm doing Grade Three, except that it seems to be the grade my school pupils all seem to try. I don't want to be doing simpler stuff than them, frankly. I couldn't live it down.'

'Hmm,' she replied. 'We shall see. So you're a teacher too? And what kind of piano do you have, Mr. Reid?'

I paused, took a deep breath, then told her. 'A Technics SX PC-26.' Actually, it was my pride and joy.

There was a long silence at the other end of the line, then a another low growling noise.

'That doesn't sound like any make of piano I've ever heard of, Mr. Reid.'

'It's an electric piano,' I confessed.

'There are pianos and electric keyboards,' she insisted. 'You seem to have one of the latter.'

'I understand you don't like them, but I live in a flat and it's only fair on the neighbours given that I'm not very good.'

For some reason this show of humility seemed to soften her. 'Ah well,' she said, 'I suppose the Good Lord sends me all sorts. If you work, you'd probably like an early evening time, on your way home. I can fit you in on Thursday at six.'

'Oh yes, thank you, Ms. Maxwell-Hume. I'll look forward to it.' It was relief, rather than pleasure, which made me say that. In truth I was wishing I'd never phoned at all.

'So will I, Mr. Reid. Let's hope we don't disappoint each other, shall we? I charge thirty pounds per lesson, by the way,' and then she gave me directions to her house.

Almost as an afterthought, she asked, 'Have you had lessons before, Mr. Reid?'

Had I had lessons before? Had I had lessons before? Oh yes.

The first piano teacher I had was actually a teacher at my school, a woman called Lex who was the head of the music department. We had a nice relationship, but I was limited to doing lessons in school, at lunchtime or at the end of the day, and neither of us was really in a position to give it our fullest commitment. Besides, she felt uncomfortable charging me anything like the going rate, and we were both aware that I was also her line manager in the school. How could she tell her boss that he was a waste of space on the piano? How could she give me a ticking off for not doing enough practice ten minutes after I'd had a go at her for being late for her class (as she often was). We got on great, but our friendships at work were too precious to both of us to allow them to be spoiled over such trivia as piano lessons. As Lex herself put it, 'this is too delicate, Brian.' Then she gave me a kiss on the cheek and a hug, and that was that.

And so I sought out professional help from the traditional sources – postcards in newsagents' shops, ads on the internet, and of course classified adverts in the local newspapers. Edinburgh – where I live in a basement flat very near to the West End, by the way – has only one local paper, the *Edinburgh Evening News*, but it has other freebies, or at least it did then – the *Herald and Post*, and – on the buses – the *Metro*. The *Evening News* offered just one option, an older, middle-class woman called Yvonne who gave over thirty lessons per week in her own home, far too close to my school. She was nice, but at work I kept hearing whispered tales of my excruciatingly bad playing. I needed more privacy than she could offer.

I found Dave through his website. Dave was a tall, incredibly thin man with thick glasses, a shaven head, an accent halfway between Essex and Edinburgh, and a pronounced lisp. He might have been gay. On my first visit, he asked me to play something – anything – so that he could judge my ability, at the conclusion of which he asked me what I would like to be able to play. When I replied, 'I really like Bach', he replied 'So do I, which is why I will never allow someone as bad as you to go anywhere near his music.' That ended my only lesson with Dave.

Martin was a student at Edinburgh university. He wasn't a music student, you understand, and he had no qualifications at all, but he played keyboards in an electronica band and was looking to supplement his student loan by giving lessons. He was the only teacher I had whose face didn't collapse on hearing that I possessed a Technics SX PC-26; he was also the only teacher who insisted that I learn to play the piano (or keyboard) standing up. ('It's how any modern band plays it, man. Sitting at a keyboard is so *out*.') Although he was prepared to teach me how to play the piano with one-finger – the left hand was for waving, punching the air, and blowing kisses to the crowd – I decided that he and I weren't quite on the same wavelength.

Then one Sunday I was walking back from the Stockbridge market when I noticed a couple of pink notices tied to a lamp-posts in a side street. Assuming they were there to announce a road closure or an increase in parking charges, I stopped to have a look, only to discover the following:

PIANO LESSONS
EXPERIENCED TEACHER
GUARANTEED SUCCESS

And then followed the name and telephone number of Mary Maxwell-Hume.

And so, four days later, I found myself en route to her house. I confess I was a little intrigued by the woman's 'guaranteed success' claim – I'd be testing that to the limit. On reflection, setting my aims and objectives at passing Grade Three piano was the equivalent of trying to scale Everest without ropes.

Mary Maxwell-Hume lived in a quiet terraced villa in the Trinity area in the north of Edinburgh, and I was forced to park my green Honda Jazz at the end of her street and walk back some distance on foot to her house. I was relieved that there was no sign of life as I made my way up the path to her front door. Ringing the bell produced no sound and no response, so I rang it again, longer this time in the hope of hearing myself, and my finger was still attached to the buzzer when the door opened. As soon as the door opened I could hear a doorbell ringing – loudly – in another room. Ah – that must be me, I thought, and sure enough removing my finger caused the noise to stop.

'Sorry,' I said. 'I thought the bell was broken.'

'Well, it's not,' the woman before me replied. That's all she said.

Whatever I was expecting my new piano teacher to look like, this wasn't it. She was tall and slim – with the benefit of the three steps up into her house she towered above me. I guessed she was around fifty, although she could have been as old as me and simply looked young for her age. Her hair contained colour and streaks of silver, but I couldn't tell how much was her own. She was wearing a dress, not any ordinary dress, but a blue calf-length lace thing that accentuated every sinewy curve of her figure from top to toe. She had discreetly-dangling earrings, she was barefoot, and she wore a sizeable quantity of some sort of perfume which didn't make me feel sick, and so therefore was probably expensive. It might have been Chanel No.5, now that I think about it.

I must have been staring open-mouthed at this apparition for almost ten seconds when she finally said, 'I assume you are Mr. Reid?' There might have been be the faintest trace of a Mona Lisa smile there.

'Yes.' It was all I could manage. Then I remembered my manners. 'Ms. Maxwell-Hume?'

'You've come to the correct place, Mr. Reid. But unless you plan on having your lesson in my front garden, I'd suggest you come in. Please leave your shoes at the front door.' As

I removed my shoes, I was at once both grateful that I put clean socks on before I left home, and curious about how I would deal with the piano pedals.

'Come through with me to the piano room.' I followed her into a large south-facing room which backed onto a conservatory and then an extensive back garden which was bathed in the summer sunlight. In the centre of the room were a couple of large traditional sofas, and looking behind me, I spotted a full-size grand piano, which I suspected might be the focus of today's activities. She motioned me to sit down on one of the sofas, then to my surprise she opted to sit at the other end of the same one.

She studied me. 'Do you like what you see?' she asked.

Mary Maxwell-Hume had put the question in the oddest way, especially as she waited until I was looking directly at her before she asked.

'Yes,' I replied, deciding to keep my options as far open as possible. 'Beautiful.'

'Call me Mary, Mr. Reid.'

'My name's Brian,' I replied. 'Brian Reid.'

'Well, Brian, this is where I give my piano lessons. And you would like to do a Grade Three exam, you say?'

'That's the idea,' I assured her.

'Then I'm sure you'll succeed. In fact I guarantee it.'

'You do?'

'Trust me, Brian,' she said firmly. 'But first I need to hear what you can do, to get some idea of the task ahead.' I was supposed to be the schoolteacher, but she was the one in control.

'How much did you say you charged?' I asked, just to be sure.

'The standard – thirty pounds.' She paused. 'For fifteen minutes.'

'What? Other teachers charge that for thirty minutes.'

'They're not as good as me. I may seem expensive, but I guarantee success.'

I tried to take this in. 'Do I get all my money back if I fail?'

'Of course. But you won't fail.'

'You haven't heard me yet. I'm not very good,' I told her.

'Which is why you really ought to start playing,' she said quietly. 'You'll be paying for my time, whether you play or not.' It was slightly sinister.

'So no coffee and biscuits beforehand?' I asked. I'd been looking forward to a Kit-Kat or a Blue Riband. All my other teachers had begun with some sort of welcome routine.

'No coffee and biscuits.'

She instructed me to play. For those who have never had a piano lesson as an adult, it's a sweat-inducingly nerve-wracking experience, and this woman had the palms of my hands utterly awash already – the soles of my feet, too. I made a note to try not to slip on her sanded wooden floor, but the bright summer light flooding in from the garden showed my footprints as I walked. It was a relief to reach the safety of the piano stool before I fainted with fear.

'I see you've brought some music with you, Brian. Is this what you've been playing?'

It was the music from the Associated Board of the Royal Schools of Music – the gold standard of music exams – Grade Three. I nodded my head. 'I've been trying to play a couple of the pieces,' I told her, but omitting the words '...for over a year.'

'Play for me,' she commanded, with a wave. She'd still not risen from the sofa. 'Perhaps you should start by playing a couple of scales for me. Would you like that? Do you practise scales, Brian? I do hope so.'

The answers to those two questions were 'no' and 'very little' respectively, but neither of those was the correct answers, so I simply replied, 'Where would you like me to start?'

'How about the key of C?'

In theory, this should be the easiest of all the keys on the piano, played as it is on all the white notes, although personally I've always found it slightly more reassuring to have the odd black note to say hello to on the way up and down. In my sweaty hands, I made a complete mess of the key of C.

'Can I try again?' I asked. 'I'm a little nervous.' She nodded, but in fact the second attempt was worse, and the third worse still after that.

'The key of C can be a little tricky, Brian,' she said, coolly. 'How about G?'

G was a little better. There's only one black note, but it helps. At Grade Three level, I only had to play two octaves, I reminded myself. On the other hand, that was sixty notes, which I had to play in the right order and on a mixture of two hands.

Next I stumbled through D, then A minor. Then she dropped the nuclear bomb on me.

'Play E flat, please.'

E flat is a complete nightmare of a key on the piano, requiring the player to engineer a thumb movement only really suited to animals with a surfeit of fingers. It took me almost thirty seconds to work my way up the two octaves of E flat and back down again.

'Hmm,' she said. I couldn't really bring myself to think of her as 'Mary'. 'Perhaps scales are not your strongest suit, Brian.'

'In terms of the piano, perhaps I'm more likely to apply

clubs and spades than hearts and diamonds,' I suggested. It was meant to be a joke, but she simply frowned at me.

'So it seems,' she replied. OK, I thought, so that joke fell flat on its face. 'How about playing some music for me, Brian? Shall we try that? What do you have?'

In fact I'd been practising a couple of things furiously, the first of which was by James Hook, an eighteenth-century English organist and composer who made lots of money by writing idiot-proof pieces for beginners. I set off playing it, pretending to follow the music, but actually as soon as I referred to the music for real, I lost my way, so I ended up playing the piece as a four-part serial. Nor was the second piece any more successful, a *Little Study in D Minor* by Theodor Kirchner, a composer I knew nothing about and cared even less. My version of his *Little Study* occasionally found the key of D minor, but only occasionally.

The end of this – I hesitate to use the word – performance – was greeted with silence by Mary Maxwell-Hume. She studied me for a moment, then uttered her judgement.

'You're not very good, are you?'

Actually, I'd thought I was a bit better than 'not very good', perhaps 'requires improvement' or even 'shows some promise', so 'not very good' was a bit of a disappointment.

'No,' I agreed. 'Is Grade Three beyond me?'

'Perhaps you need to broaden your horizons,' she suggested.

'What did you have in mind?'

'The Associated Board isn't the only organisation that offers piano exams.'

'Isn't it?'

'Not at all. There are also the Trinity Guildhall exams, and the London Colleges offer exams, too. There's even Rockschool, which does exams for playing rock music.'

'Really?' I perked up, 'Rock sounds fun.'

'It's also very hard, and horrible to listen to. But anyway, I have another suggestion. I think we should consider the British School of Music's exams. I like them best anyway, but I also believe you could pass Grade Three in the BSM's syllabus.'

'Is it easier?'

'Not at all. It's just that the BSM looks for different qualities in its candidates. They're less concerned with technique, more with musicality. The scales and arpeggios don't count so much.'

'Sounds good.'

'On the other hand the British School of Music asks its candidates to be more musical.' She leaned across to a side table and picked up a small purple-covered booklet I hadn't noticed before. 'Page four of the BSM syllabus here says that 'candidates will be assessed on their ability to impress the examiner with their sense of musicality. Candidates should choose at least one piece that the examiner is unlikely to have heard before, and to perform it in such a way that the examiner is likely to want to hear it again."

'Wow,' I said. 'How on earth do I do that? And how do I find a piece that the examiner is unlikely to have heard before? Write it myself?'

'That would be one possibility, but are you up to that?'

'No.' Then a thought came to me. 'What about that piece where the pianist sits and plays nothing at all? They won't have heard that, I suppose.' It was another attempt to lighten the mood. I actually thought it was quite funny, but once again it failed completely.

'*4.33* by John Cage,' she said, utterly seriously. 'Complete silence, but harder for beginners than it seems. Most play it either too fast or too slow.'

She continued to study me, then that Mona Lisa smile returned. 'Might I suggest you might use something from my library of lesser-known piano pieces?'

To say I was surprised at this would be an understatement. 'You have such a thing?'

'Certainly.' She reached behind her again, and this time produced a black A4 ring-binder which proved to be full of printed piano music. 'They're arranged here by difficulty, Grade One through to Grade Eight. I have a few here at Grade Three level.' She reached into the folder and handed me a piece of paper. 'How about this one?'

It was just a jumble of notes, of course. The piece was entitled *Study In A Flat* and its composer appeared to be 'M. M. Hume'.

'You wrote this?' I asked her.

'Yes. I should play it for you, shouldn't I, to let you hear how it should sound?'

I wasn't given a chance to reply. Insisting I didn't need to get up, she sat beside me on the stool, relieved me of the music and transferred it to the music rest on the piano itself. It was quite a long piano stool, so there was plenty of room for both of us, but her need to get as near to the middle of the keyboard pushed her body into the closest contact with mine. And of course there was that perfume.

Mary Maxwell-Hume seemed quite immune to any discomfort I might be feeling as she played the piece, a slow waltz which had a simple tune and a quiet left hand accompaniment. When she finished, I had to admit that I rather liked it. But it seemed a little hard and it was written in A flat, which is a very difficult key indeed for Grade Three. I told her that I wasn't sure that I could manage it.

'Oh but you *must*,' she insisted. 'The one thing you must do is let my music be heard.' Then she said firmly again, studying the music rather than me, 'You will do this, Brian. You will.'

'I can try.'

She instructed me to try immediately, at a couple of points even physically placing my hands in particular positions on the keys. Of course it was a disaster, but once I'd played it a couple of times with her on the stool beside me, she returned to her sofa and asked me to play it once through as a 'concert' performance, taking care not to stop. I didn't stop, but the sound that emerged from her lovely piano was something similar to the sound the refuse men make emptying my rubbish into their lorry.

'I'd like you to take it home and practise it, and come back next week. Practise the other two pieces as well – you'll need all three for the exam.' Then suddenly she changed tack. 'Are you fortunate enough to have any family, Brian?'

It was the first personal thing we had discussed. I briefly explained that I was recently divorced and that I had two grown-up children, but I told it succinctly, given that the tale was costing me two pounds per minute. Even BT's Helpline is cheaper.

'What about you?' I asked her.

'No. Just me. I'm fine with that.' It was a minimalist reply, and it seemed to mark the end of the lesson. Mary Maxwell-Hume announced that I was due her ninety pounds for forty-five minutes' worth of piano lesson – around sixty pounds more than I was expecting to pay – and that she was looking forward to seeing me at the same time next week. No doubt.

As we made for the front door – there was a moment's delay as I wrestled my shoes back on – I was aware that she couldn't charge me any more for time spent in small talk. I took the opportunity to spear in another personal question.

'Do you teach piano full-time, Mary, or do you have a day-job as well?'

'Yes and no,' she replied. 'I'm a nun. I regard that as my 'day-job', if you wish to see it that way. Some might not.' My jaw must have been dropping too obviously, because she carried on, 'Not all nuns dress the same way, Brian. I belong to the order of the Sisters of Mary of the Sacred Cross.'

I'd never heard of them, but that didn't mean much. 'So your order believes you should dress in the same way as everyone else?'

'Not quite, Brian. Clothing should not act as an adornment of the body, and we believe we should only wear what is necessary to provide due modesty.'

'I see.' Actually, I wasn't sure that I did.

I *did* put some effort into my piano practice.

The following Thursday at six, I presented myself at Mary's front door, which opened to reveal the same Mona Lisa smile, the same hair, the same lack of shoes, the same Chanel No.5; only the dress had altered. This time she wore a light cotton print which – against the strong sunlight streaming through the conservatory window – perhaps revealed a little more of her lithe form than was appropriate for a music teacher or a nun, far less both. But I wased too polite to do any more than look away. The scales needed more attention, she declared, the Hook was 'clunky' and the Kirchner has improved, she said, to 'awful'. She listened to her own piece patiently, but declared it to be 'rather ordinary'. I suggested that 'rather ordinary' represents a huge improvement, but she would have none of it. She demanded 'exceptional'. So I was sent away with a long list of things to work on, and a wallet another ninety pounds lighter.

Exactly one week later, almost everything was identical again, and if the elegant ankle-length black silk dress she was wearing wasn't see-through in any way this time, it somehow allowed for even greater contact as she joined me at the piano stool to demonstrate one or two aspects of each piece to me. She chose this moment to spring a surprise.

'Now, Brian, I have some news for you. I've entered you for the Grade Three exam.'

I was genuinely shocked. 'But am I ready? Surely not?'

'No, but you will be by the time of the exam,' she reassured me.

'When will that be?'

'A fortnight tonight, six o'clock.'

'A *fortnight*?'

'The exam will be held in the church hall down at the end of the road,' she added, with the Mona Lisa smile. You pass it as you come down the road each time.'

'I need to do masses of work, surely,' I said in panic.

'You do. We do, Brian. We need to spend a good while tonight, for a start.'

I pointed out that this was costing me a lot of money.

'But that's why we need to present you for the exam so soon, Brian. Remember if you fail, I give you all your money back. By the way, the exam itself costs seventy-five pounds to enter. Cash.'

This was getting worse. 'I give it to you now? I don't have that sort of money on me, Mary.'

She looked at me as if I were a five year old. 'Of course not. You pay the examiner. If you want the results on the day, by the way, there's a surcharge of twenty-five pounds.'

'A hundred in total, in other words.'

'Indeed. Or else the results can take several months.'

I didn't have to pay the entry fee that night, but by the

time we'd finished, my lesson had set me back one hundred and twenty pounds.

My last lesson, then, was to be a mere four weeks after Mary Maxwell-Hume and I had first met. Outside her door, I paused for a moment to wonder what awaited me, although I should have been prepared by now. It opened to reveal: a barefoot, tall, slim figure, delicate earrings, hair as before and with a Mona Lisa smile. The dress, however, was calf-length, deep red, and made of an expensive cotton crepe that gave and stretched with every part of her body. As I followed her through to the living room, I became acutely aware that anything worn under the dress would now be showing through it. Except that nothing was.

She turned around and caught me looking at her.

'Is everything all right, Brian? You've forgotten to remove your shoes.' she asked. The Mona Lisa smile was still there.

In my fumbling confusion to rectify my error, I blurted it out. 'Sorry. I was admiring your dress, Mary. It's lovely – I mean it's a lovely colour.'

'It's functional,' she replied. Then I remembered. *We believe we should only wear what is necessary to provide due modesty.*

Mary had already warned me that this would need to be an intensive session, so without further ado she had me play through all the scales and a couple of arpeggios. It was slow, but the mistakes had decreased. Then I moved on to the James Hook piece, which remained 'clunky' she said, but she encouraged me to play it a little slower for accuracy, and in the end I played it three times, whereupon she declared it 'ready'. The Kirchner had improved massively with practice, and was now almost up to 'poor standard', she said. However, I ought to be comforted by the fact that standards were not high and might even, in the opinion of Mary Maxwell-Smith, be declining. I wasn't sure if that reassured me or not. I played it only twice. I suspect that was because it was as much as she could stand.

Then we came to *Study In A Flat*. I really had tried to practise this piece hard, but although I liked it, I was aware that playing anything in A Flat was just a step too far at this early stage in my piano career. Mary listened to me stumbling through it twice, then she shrugged her shoulders.

'You can only do your best, Brian.'

'And if I fail, I get my money back?'

'I'm sure you'll pass,' she said.

'You're so confident,' I said to her. 'I don't know how you can do it. If I were teaching me, I'd have given up on me long ago,' I explained, wondering if that made any sense at all.

'Ah yes, but I have a trump card,' she announced. And with that, she came to sit beside me on the piano stool, the first time tonight that she'd been that close in that red dress. She was very close anyway, but now she took my hand for good measure.

'Let us pray, Brian.'

I had absolutely no idea how to react to this, so I just went along as she closed her eyes and said quietly, 'Heavenly Father, grant thy servant Brian all thy grace in his piano exam next Thursday. Be with him as plays his scales and arpeggios, plays the work of Hook and Kirchner, and give him the strength to move the examiner as he performs *Study In A Flat*. Amen.'

There was little more that I could do other than say 'Amen', too, although I did manage to thank her in a bemused sort of way.

'You will do well, Brian. But I think we're done tonight, and our session has lasted one-and-a-half hours. That'll be one hundred and eighty pounds, please. Cash, if you don't mind.'

It was as well that I'd made an extra visit to the cash machine on the way to her house. The money was handed over, and then we made our way to the door and my shoes.

'Good luck, Brian,' she says, shaking my hand. 'Do well.'

'I promise to do my best. Shall I let you know how I get on?'

'There won't be a need. You *will* pass, Brian. God will be at your side,' she insisted, as she closed the door behind me for the final time.

Each evening in the week that followed I spent two hours practising the various aspects of the exam. I even spent some time on scales, so that by the day of the exam the major keys of C, D and G were reasonable, as were the minors in A and E, although the rest ranged from poor to the entirely hopeless E flat. I lived in hope the examiner wouldn't ask me to play it, and if he did, it wouldn't count for too much. After all, that's why I was doing the British School of Music's piano exams. I could play the two better-known pieces without too many stops, but they didn't sound anything like the recordings I'd downloaded to my iPod. I'd also discovered that people record themselves playing this sort of thing on YouTube. These sounded great to me – a six-year-old played the Hook in one clip quite brilliantly – and they get (mostly encouraging) feedback as well. By comparison I was awful, that's the truth of it. Mercifully, the *Study In A Flat* was unknown, so apart from Mary Maxwell-Hume's own private performances, I'd nothing to compare myself with.

Fortunately, that Thursday proved to be a busy day at my school, taken up largely with a major fight in the playground involving nine biting and scratching girls, so I had little chance to get nervous. But as I left the building and headed for my Honda Jazz in the car park, my legs immediately turned to jelly, and my hands were already sweating as I started the car and turned the steering wheel to head for Trinity. The heavy traffic simply heightened my blood pressure and a visit to the usual cash machine – two hundred pounds withdrawn, just to be on safe side – meant that I arrived at the exam venue with less than five minutes to spare.

As Mary had promised, it was actually a church hall on the corner of her street, less than two hundred yards from her own house, and I fleetingly wondered if at that very moment she might be on her knees at the piano praying for me to do well. If her guarantee was to hold good, she stood to lose almost five hundred pounds in repaid tuition fees, although I realised that I was so bad that I wasn't sure I'd be able to face her again. One half of the double doors of the church hall was open, while the other sported a green sheet of A4 paper attached with BlueTac with the words 'Music Exam' and an arrow pointing inside. The exam, it seemed, would not be held in the hall itself, but in a meeting room off a corridor up the side, and a couple of empty chairs were waiting for me outside.

Sitting on one, I could hear the faint sound of the piano playing. I wasn't sure it was all that good, but I was sure that the player was miles better than me, and probably about eight years old. It was therefore rather a surprise when, after a period of silence, the door opened and an older man, round and balding, emerged with a wide smile and carrying some music and a certificate.

'The examiner asks if you could just please give her a moment and then she'll call you in,' he said to me. 'She's very nice, actually,' he assured me. 'Good luck.'

I thanked him with a nod and a nervous smile in reply.

So – the examiner was female? A minute or so later, there was a call: 'Brian Reid?' and I stood up and walked through.

It was a bright, airy room, far brighter than the church hall itself. In the centre of the room stood a grand piano, my instrument of execution, bathed in evening sunlight like a guillotine. But it took me a moment to sit down because the examiner wasn't looking me, she was seated at a table at the side of the room, deeply engrossed in writing up notes either on the previous candidate, or on me. By the way, she was a nun, fully dressed in a red habit – cowl, wimple, the lot – and sitting sideways on to me with her head down, so that I could see no part of her, not even her face. After a moment I caught a glimpse of her toes. I wondered if she might be barefoot.

Without looking up, she said, 'Good afternoon, Mr. Reid. I gather you're attempting Grade Three, and you would like your results today. Is that correct?'

'Yes.'

'That'll be one hundred pounds, please. Cash. Could you just lay it on the table please while I make out a receipt and complete this form for you?'

I did as I was told. The voice was faintly familiar. As I said farewell to five twenty pound notes, I was vaguely aware of Chanel No.5, but I was so nervous and confused that I realised that my imagination might well have been playing tricks with me. The money disappeared into a bag below the table, leaving me standing before her as she continued to make notes.

'Make yourself comfortable at the piano, please,' she commanded, and I obeyed.

'Now,' the examiner said, referring to what I assumed was my entry form in front of her, 'I gather you will be playing the Hook and the Kirchner from the approved list, and then you'll play a piece for me by M. M. Hume.' Then she looked up at me for the first time. 'Is that correct?'

To begin with, I was speechless. Surely it couldn't be? It was the same... No, my nerves were confusing me and in any case all I could see of this woman was a very small circle around her face. They probably all looked the same that way, which I'm sure was the whole point. Anyway, I had an exam to pass.

'Is that correct, Mr. Reid?' she repeated. She gave me a Mona Lisa smile that seemed vaguely familiar. 'By the way, my name is Sister Mary.'

'Sorry,' I said 'It's nice to meet you, too, Sister Mary, and, yes, that's correct.'

'Shall we commence?' Again, it wasn't really a question. I nodded. 'Let's start with some scales, shall we? I'd like you begin with the key of C. Take your time – you have thirty seconds.'

Thirty seconds? That was one note every second. I played the scale very slowly indeed on the way up, took care at the top, then even slower on the way down. Sister Mary smiled enigmatically.

'Thank you,' she said. 'Now, how about the scale of G?'

The key of G has one sharp. Even I could manage that in half a minute, but I took nothing for granted and proceeded at a funeral pace. Surely the dreaded E flat must follow soon?

'Now the key of D,' she said, not even looking up.

I was almost caught out because D and E flat are next to each other on the piano, and I almost played the wrong note to start with. But I used my thirty seconds and played the scale correctly.

'And finally a minor key.' Maybe this was it. 'How about E minor?'

I could hardly believe this. It was just about the easiest one she could ask for. I played E minor carefully, slowly, but

– I suppose – otherwise perfectly.

'Well done, Mr. Reid,' she said. 'That concludes your scales. And the British School of Music doesn't always demand that candidates play arpeggios if their scales are sound. Yours are excellent, so we can move on to your pieces, I think.'

I could hardly believe it – these exercises were my weak point and she was telling me I could skip them altogether. I liked this exam.

'Now I'd like you to play a piece for me. How about trying the James Hook? Any time you're ready. We've plenty of time.'

And so I played James Hook's *Tempo di Minuetto* from *Guida di Musica*, opus 37, to the best of my ability, which wasn't very good, but in truth I couldn't do much better. Then I followed up with Theodor Kirchner's *Little Study in D minor*, opus 71, number 18, which, buoyed by the success of previous parts of my exam, managed to sound less excruciating than I'd ever made it sound before. Each piece received a quiet smile and a 'Thank you, Mr. Reid'.

'Now I'd like you to play your nominated special piece, Mr. Reid, which will be judged for its overall musicality rather than on technique. I see you have chosen a piece by M. M. Hume. Do you know anything about – him?' she asked. The Mona Lisa smile was there again.

'It's a 'she', actually. M. M. Hume is my piano teacher,' I told her.

'Excellent,' she said, and sat back as if to enjoy the music. Poor her, I thought.

But I played the piece, wishing an inward wish for Ms. Maxwell-Hume at the same time, because I did quite like playing it anyway.

A minute or so later, it was all over. I turned to look at

the examiner, who to my surprise was – I think – brushing a tear from her eye.

'Are you all right?' I asked. 'Have I upset you?'

She shook her head. 'Quite the reverse. It was beautiful. I've never heard such a beautiful piece.'

I didn't quite know what to say. 'Thank you' was about the best I could manage.

She turned her attention to the papers in front of her, and furiously scribbled lots of notes on my entry form, another sheet, and then finally signed everything. Eventually, she looked up at me.

'Mr. Reid, I'm delighted to inform you that you have passed Grade Three Piano at the British School of Music, and passed with distinction. If you'd care to step across here, I'll present you with your certificate.' She rose from her chair to greet me with a slightly wider version of the Mona Lisa smile, offering me a signed certificate with her left hand, and her right hand to shake. 'Perhaps you'd like to attempt Grade Four some time soon?'

I could hardly see any of her beneath her habit, of course, but what I could pick out of her tall, willowy figure was uncannily familiar. As was the Chanel No.5.

Accepting my coveted certificate – the signature was illegible – and shaking her hand, I asked, 'I wonder, might we have met before? You're not by any chance from the order of the Sisters of Mary of the Sacred Cross, are you?'

The Mona Lisa smile replied before she spoke. She seemed surprised. 'You've heard of us? That's nice.'

'My piano teacher happened to be of your order, as it happens.'

'My,' she said, 'what a coincidence.'

'She doesn't wear a red habit, though, she dresses… normally, if you know what I mean. The red habit is quite striking, isn't it?'

'It's functional. We believe we should only wear what is necessary to provide due modesty.' I thought I understood what that meant now, although where the Chanel No.5 fitted in, I couldn't quite fathom.

Gathering my things together to make my exit, I said, 'As far as Grade Four goes, Sister Mary, I think I might take a break from exams for a while. Perhaps in the future, though.'

'I do hope so,' she said. 'You seem to have found an excellent teacher. You must let her know that you did so well.'

'I'll phone her straight away to tell her the good news.'

But making my way from the church hall towards my Honda Jazz, I reflected on the cost of passing Grade Three piano in the British School of Music and suspected that I could at least save myself the price of a phone call.

*****

Study in A Flat
(British School of Music Grade 3 piano examination piece)

M. M. Hume

Andante (♩=100)

Acknowledgements

This collection of stories owes everything to Bruce Levine, an extraordinarily multi-talented musician, composer, musical director, actor and writer. Bruce and I have never met, never even spoken on the telephone. I first came across him through our mutual interest in Friday Flash Fiction. He kindly read each of these stories, and acted as my initial proofreader. Thanks, Bruce. Fellow Comely Bank Publishing authors Emma Baird (*Katie And The Deelans*, *The Girl Who Swapped*) and Jane Tulloch (*Our Best Attention*, *Assured Attention*) also made encouraging noises. Thereafter, Dougie Dalgleish went through the entire thing forensically, picking out even more of my typos, together with the odd unintelligible section, and my thanks are due to him, too. Joseph White cast his usual expert eye over the cover. But in the end, all the mistakes and typing errors are my responsibility and mine alone.

One other person needs to be thanked – my wife Katherine, for her limitless patience (and yet more proofreading). An honourable mention goes to Finn and Orla, too, for occasionally allowing me to think on Wednesdays in between feeding and watering them, playing with Lego, reading stories, playing games, and generally playing whatever role Grandpa is allocated at any given moment.

About The Author

Born in 1952, Gordon Lawrie has lived and worked all his life in Edinburgh. Until 2011, he was a Modern Studies - politics, for the uninitiated - teacher in a very large secondary school in a very inappropriate high-rise building.

Seizing an opportunity for a career change in 2011, he tried his hand at writing fiction. He struck... well perhaps not gold, some baser metal instead, with *Four Old Geezers And A Valkyre*, a romantic comedy about four sad superannuated wannabe rockstars who accidentally have a couple of YouTube hits.

Gordon is also a prolific short story writer and essayist, as well as an occasional poet and journalist. He is also a flash fiction writer, specialising in the 'drabble' form which is exactly 100 words long. In 2016 he published *100 Not Out*, a first collection of the best of them.

Gordon's second published novel, *The Blogger Who Came In From The Cold*, is due to be released in 2018.

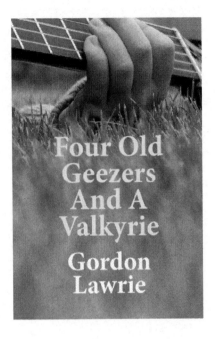

Brian Reid – aka 'Captain' – is a retired, newly-divorced ex-teacher in financial and personal crisis. When his best man re-enters his life and persuades Captain to pick up his long-abandoned guitar, the resulting band of superannuated misfits record a couple of songs which become surprise YouTube hits.

The new rockstars face a problem, however: the image of the band that their manager has created is completely at odds with the real thing. As a result they can't do any live concerts. Or can they?

About Comely Bank Publishing

Comely Bank Publishing (CBP) is a co-operative publishing house giving bright, new talent a platform.

Founded in 2012, CBP aims to tackle the quality issues faced by traditional publishing, i.e. the concentration on books only by established authors or bankable names. CPB helps new authors publish at low cost and makes no profits from its authors.

Comedy, historical fiction, young adult fiction and more – Comely Bank Publishing covers many genres and we are sure you will find a book you enjoy…

All books are available in print and e-book formats on Amazon, Kobo and other outlets, as well as in Edinburgh bookshops and directly from the Comely Bank Publishing website:

http//www.comelybankpublishing.com